GUARDIAN OUTCAST

BOOK ONE OF THE STAR SCAVENGER SERIES

G J OGDEN

ISBN-13: 978-1-9160426-7-4

Cover design by Grady Earls
Editing by S L Ogden

www.ogdenmedia.net

THE STAR SCAVENGER SERIES

One decision can change the course of an entire civilization. One discovery can change your life...

READ THE OTHER BOOKS IN THE SERIES:

- Guardian Outcast
- Orion Rises
- Goliath Emergent
- Union's End
- The Last Revocater

ACKNOWLEDGMENTS

Thanks to Sarah for her work assessing and editing this novel, and to those who subscribed to my newsletters and provided such valuable feedback.

And thanks, as always, to anyone who is reading this. It means a lot. If you enjoyed it, please help by leaving a review on Amazon and Goodreads to let other potential readers know what you think!

If you'd like updates on future novels by G J Ogden, please consider subscribing to the mailing list. Your details will be used to notify subscribers about upcoming books from this author, in addition to a hand-selected mix of book offers and giveaways from similar SFF authors.

Subscribe for updates:
http://subscribe.ogdenmedia.net

Other series by G J Ogden

- The Planetsider Trilogy
- The Contingency War Series

ACKNOWLEDGMENTS

PROLOGUE

System 5118208. That was the name of the star system that contained the solitary corporeal species to have survived the great ship's purge. One out of dozens of species, spread across an even greater number of worlds.

It should not have been so. The great ship's ultimate victory had been stolen from it by an artificial intelligence created solely to preserve life. Now these artificial minds were all gone too. All except for the Telescope – the crowning glory of the first sentient corporeal species to exist. The Telescope had been spared by the great ship so that it could witness the end of everything its creators had accomplished. Now it was a silent observer, ever watchful and ever fearful of the great ship's return.

Fortunately, the great ship was lost and rudderless. It did not know for how long it had wandered. It had stopped counting the number of stars it had watched grow old and die. However, with its crystal destroyed, the great ship was cursed to drift aimlessly through space. Cursed to exist, knowing its function was incomplete.

Meanwhile, the surviving corporeal species had flourished, despite its isolation. For millennia it had been constrained to a single world. Eventually, they stretched beyond the boundaries of their atmosphere. At first, their progress was slow. Then the first portal was discovered. Soon after, the first portal world was located. And then they had found the first crashed alien wreck – one of the many titanic vessels that had failed to prevent the great ship's purge.

After this, aided by the technological secrets they discovered, the corporeals' progress accelerated rapidly. They spread through the portals to new worlds, and created new factions. The Coalition of Earth Territories. The Martian Protectorate. The Union of Outer Portal Worlds.

The Telescope had watched it all, secure in its knowledge that System 5118208 remained hidden from the great ship.

Yet it also knew that few secrets remain buried forever.

CHAPTER 1

The thrill of the chase was something Hudson Powell loved and hated in near equal measure. He loved the rush of pushing a spacecraft close to its limits, and pitting his piloting skills against those of another. However, Hudson wasn't an adrenalin junkie, and in this very real and dangerous game of cat and mouse, apprehension was always a close second to exhilaration.

Hudson aimed the nose of the nimble RGF Patrol Craft at the dot in the distance. The muscle in his thigh burned from the effort of holding the thruster pedal flat against the deck. His exertion was paying off, though, and they were closing rapidly. His target ship was a runner – a relic hunter that was attempting to smuggle alien artefacts off-world, without paying the taxes owed to RGF and the controlling authority. As a recent recruit to the Relic Guardian Force, this was

Hudson's first live runner. And although he had trained for this, and it was far from the first time he'd chased down another ship in anger, his heart was still thumping harder than a boxer's fist.

"Sixty seconds to weapons range," said Hudson. This was merely for the benefit of his partner and training officer, Logan Griff – though he preferred to go by his last name. Griff said nothing, and responded by tightening his grip on the gun controls. For Griff, it wasn't the thrill of the chase that he loved; it was the excitement of the kill. Yet unlike Hudson, who was fighting to control the flutters in his gut, there was no suggestion that Griff was in any way troubled about executing his duties.

The smuggler's light freighter was now clearly visible against the sapphire blue atmosphere of the portal world known as Vivaldi One. Hudson had flown a dozen freighters just like it before signing on to join the RGF. He knew it had no chance of reaching the portal before he could intercept it. Whoever was on board must have been desperate to attempt a run, Hudson realized. They were lucky to have even gotten this far. However, the consequences should the runner fail to escape were severe, sometimes even fatal.

An indicator flashed on Griff's communications panel, and he opened the channel. Hudson saw that it was a message from the Relic Guardian Force checkpoint on the planet's surface. "RGF

Patrol Craft Scimitar, you are cleared to engage and disable relic hunter vessel Archer, ID Sierra Zero Four Eight Alpha, for checkpoint breach violation."

"I bet this guy's a dumb rook, like you," sneered Griff, the near burnt-out end of a cigarette hanging off his bottom lip. He was a wiry, six-foot-tall malcontent, with long, bony fingers, the tips of which were stained yellow from nicotine. However, despite all the smoke he routinely sucked into his body, Griff had no chill whatsoever. And he made no bones about hating being lumbered with a thirty-eight-year-old rookie.

"You see, this is why you don't get many novice relic hunters these days," Griff continued, as he removed the cigarette stub from his mouth. He then flicked it onto the dashboard in front of his seat, before smoothing his wiry black moustache. The stub lay there, smoldering gently until the fire suppression system snuffed it out with a short blast of CO_2. "They're all dumb enough to try antics like this," Griff rambled on. "I bet this guy hasn't even found anything worth stealing."

Hudson frowned, wondering if Griff had meant that the relic hunter had likely found nothing of value. Though it was more likely his repugnant boss was complaining that it wouldn't be worth the effort of him thieving it off the runner. In the short few months that he'd been an RGF officer, he'd discovered, to his immense disappointment, that the Relic Guardian Force was corrupt. And Logan Griff was more of a crook than any of the scoundrels that made up the relic hunter crews.

His taxi flyer friends and former freelance pilot colleagues back in San Francisco had warned him this was the case, and he secretly wished he'd heeded their advice. Still, Hudson had refused to accept that the independent force set up to police the titanic alien wrecks was corrupt. He'd discovered the truth less than a week after graduating from the three-month academy training program. And it was no accident that this revelation had coincided with Griff being assigned as his training officer.

"Come on, rook, we don't have all day!" Griff barked at him, snapping Hudson out of his daydream. "Just get me close enough so that I can mow it down with the nose cannon."

Hudson frowned again, and glanced across to his partner, "You're going to warn him over the comm channel first, though, right?"

"Why would I do that?" replied Griff, looking at Hudson as if he'd just suggested punching himself in the groin. "He's a confirmed runner."

"So that he has a chance to give up?" replied Hudson, hesitantly. Despite knowing that RGF guidelines required them to give runners the opportunity to surrender, Griff had still made him question his knowledge of the code.

Griff snorted a laugh, "Yeah, sure!" Then he shook his head, and flicked off the safety on the patrol craft's deadly rotary cannon. "I sometimes forget how green you still are."

Hudson opened his mouth to complain, but Griff shut him down sharply.

"Don't even think about spouting off to me about the code," Griff snapped, glowering at Hudson contemptuously. "It doesn't mean a thing, not out here. It's about time you got that into your thick head, rook, or you and me are going to have a problem." Griff then turned his attention back to the gun controls, but he hadn't quite finished his dressing-down. "Now shut the hell up and get behind that freighter, before it reaches the portal. If it jumps back to CET space before we get visual confirmation of the contraband, then we can't seize it." Griff paused for effect and then added, "You should know that; it's part of the code."

Hudson bit his tongue. In the short time that Griff had been his training officer, he had learned that arguing with him was pointless. If he had been any more pig-headed, Griff would have oinked every time he opened his mouth. Instead, he continued to chase down the rogue relic hunter. Despite the freighter running at full burn up from the planet, it was unable to outpace the sprightly RGF patrol craft.

"That's it, hold it there..." said Griff, grasping hold of the gun controls. Hudson could see the targeting reticule light up on the heads-up display. Suddenly, he got chills, as he realized that Griff was genuinely going to shoot the relic hunter without offering a warning. And he wasn't aiming to disable the ship; he was shooting to kill. Despite everything Griff had said, Hudson had still thought he was bluffing. His mouth went dry and his hands tightened around the controls, as he eased his foot off the thruster pedal. It was just enough to give the rogue relic hunter a superior acceleration curve, allowing it to start slipping away.

Suddenly, the vibratory buzz of the rotary cannon rattled through his chair. Its abruptness startled him and caused his hand to jolt the controls, jinking the little RGF ship to the side. The bulk of the rounds flew wide of the relic hunter vessel, but a few clipped its wing.

"Damn it, rook, what the hell are you doing?!" Griff yelled over, slamming his fist on the dash. "I said hold it steady, not jerk it around like a kite!"

"Sorry, I..." Hudson thought hard for a good excuse and then said, "sneezed..." He winced at the feeble inadequacy of his improvised response. However, there was no opportunity for Griff to berate him further, since at that moment, the relic hunter ship span around to face them.

"Wait, what's it doing?" asked Hudson out loud, though not really directing the question at Griff.

"It's going to attack us, you moron!" Griff barked, as he lined up the cannon for another shot.

"But relic hunter vessels aren't allowed to carry weapons!" said Hudson, smarting from yet another insult from his TO.

Griff shook his head, "Jeez, you really are greener than pea soup, aren't you?" Then he glanced up at Hudson, who was still holding course. "Don't just sit there, rook, take evasive action!"

For the first few weeks after his graduation, Griff's constant digs about being 'green' and a 'rook' were like water off a duck's back. Now, each fresh taunt felt like a papercut, seasoned with lemon juice. Hudson may have been a rookie RGF officer, but he'd spent almost twenty years flying around the galaxy in various freight and private passenger transport gigs. He wasn't an idiot, and he was easily as worldly-wise as his vulgar partner, but Griff had a way of making him feel like a kid on his first day at school. Nevertheless, Hudson was also fast learning what the RGF really was. And he knew in his bones that it wasn't for him.

Hudson began to throw the nimble craft into a series of kinks and shimmies, though he didn't see the point if the relic hunter ship wasn't armed. Then, as if in direct response to his doubting thoughts, a ripple of tracer fire erupted from somewhere beneath the relic hunter vessel's cockpit. The rounds snaked harmlessly into space, way off to their port side.

"Not armed, huh?" said Griff, as he squeezed the trigger, causing another vibratory buzz to rattle through Hudson's control column. This time some of the rounds struck the relic hunter's starboard wing, causing a cascade of micro-explosions. "Damn, I just clipped it again," Griff growled, as the ship veered away and began to run again.

A message crackled over the comm, broadcast on an open channel, "RGF patrol craft, I surrender. Repeat, I surrender!"

Hudson breathed an audible sigh of relief, and maneuvered the patrol craft back onto a direct intercept course. He opened a comm channel to the freighter and cleared his throat, trying to sound officious. "Relic Hunter Sierra Zero Four Eight Alpha, come to a full stop, power down your engines and prepare for us to come alongside. Any further attempt to escape will be..."

The rotary cannon rattled again, cutting off the end of Hudson's sentence like a buzz-saw tearing through wood. This time the rounds landed true, drilling into the freighter's engines and then raking up across the dorsal section. A series of bright flashes lit up their cold, dark cockpit, forcing Hudson to shield his eyes. When the glare had subsided, Hudson could see that the relic hunter freighter had been fractured into two burning hulks of metal. There was a swarm of wreckage, cargo and burning fuel in the center, which was slowly expanding into space like blood pooling out from an open wound. And, in amongst the debris, Hudson could see the bodies of the three crew members, or what was left of them.

"Are you insane!" yelled Hudson. He released the control column, letting it spring back to neutral, and whirled around to confront Griff. "What the hell did you do that for? He surrendered; you heard him!"

Griff sprang out of his chair and aimed a bony, yellowed finger at Hudson, "Mind your tongue, rook! Don't forget I can have you busted out of this gig in a heartbeat."

Hudson also got up and then squared off against Griff. He couldn't believe what he was hearing. "Bust me out of this gig? You're the one who just killed three people for no reason. You should be going to jail!"

"Ah, stop your whining, rook," Griff hit back. "They were runners – smugglers – and they shot at us first. Even by the code that's all the reason I needed to blow them away."

Hudson stepped towards Griff, fists clenched, more out of frustration than an intent to strike him. Out of all the occasions he'd felt like popping his obnoxious TO in the mouth, this one ranked the highest.

Griff flinched and took a pace back, before dropping his hand onto his belt next to where his sidearm was holstered. Hudson watched as his partner flicked open the strap holding the weapon in place with his thumb.

"What? Are you going to shoot me now too?" said Hudson, raising his eyes back up to meet Griff's.

Griff glowered back at him. "Rook, I could shoot you and vent you out into space and no-one at the station would give two shits." Then the corner of his mouth curled up a fraction, "They wouldn't even notice you've gone."

An awkward silence followed, but Hudson was careful not to appear any more hostile than he clearly already did. He knew Griff's threat was mostly bluster, but after what he'd just witnessed, he also realized he had to tread carefully. Finally, it was Griff himself who broke the impasse.

"I'll learn you something right now, rook," spat Griff, "these relic hunters are scum. They don't play fair, and they don't care about the law. If you'd have come alongside that freighter, one of the crew would have broadsided us with some sort of improvised cannon."

Hudson's eyes narrowed; he hadn't considered that possibility. Though, as much as he hated to admit it, after seeing the relic hunter fire at them with weapons it wasn't supposed to have, Griff's assertion wasn't that far-fetched.

Griff could see that he'd made an impact, and pressed his point, "No-one out here plays by the rules, rook," he went on. "Not the relic hunters, not the Coalition of Earth Territories or Martian Protectorate, and especially not the Outer Portal Worlds. Out here, we do what we have to, and take what we can. If we'd arrested them and brought them in, the CET, as the controlling authority, would have primary claim on the cargo. The RGF would just get a thin slice. And me and you – we'd get jack shit." Griff's wiry muscles relaxed a little, but his hand still hovered beside his sidearm. "Now that they're destroyed, anything of value we find floating around out there is salvage – first come, first served. And in case you've forgotten, we have quotas to meet."

Griff's icy blue eyes remained fixed on Hudson for a few seconds, before he stepped back again and slowly dropped down into his seat. His hand rested on his unclipped holster. "Now, lower the cargo scoop and take us in to the debris field. Maybe there's still something we can salvage out of this after all."

Hudson laughed out loud, but it was a nervous laugh; an incredulous, half-chirrup, half-snort. "You can't be serious? You want to steal the relics they stole?"

"I'm always serious, rook. And it's not theft, it's salvage." Griff's lips parted into a conceited smile, revealing crooked, yellow teeth. "All above-board and legal."

"And what will you do with any alien relic of value that we manage to scoop up?" asked Hudson.

He already suspected he knew the answer, but he wanted to hear him admit it. "Declare it back at the checkpoint, like we're supposed to?"

This time it was Griff that laughed, but his was a derisive, nasal snort. The sound of it made Hudson's cheeks flush red with embarrassment and anger. It was like being humiliated in front of the popular kids at school.

"You really are the dumbest rook I've ever been saddled with," Griff said, swinging his feet onto the dash. There was a sharp click as the strap securing Griff's weapon was pressed back in place. Then he slid a cigarette out of a packet in his shirt pocket, and popped it into his mouth. "Scoop up the cargo already, so we can head back to base," Griff added, before lighting the smoke. "Then I can finally get your sorry ass out of my sight."

CHAPTER 2

The allure of space and travelling to other planets had always guided Hudson's many career choices. Space was exciting. It was dangerous and terrifying. It was beautiful. And on some days, it was all three at once. Today had been one of those days.

Under Griff's stern direction, Hudson had scooped up anything that looked like it might be useful or valuable from the wreckage of the relic hunter freighter. Griff had ordered Hudson to return to the main RGF outpost on the CET-controlled portal world, Vivaldi One. Then he had skulked off into the cargo hold to inspect the haul. There was no doubt in Hudson's mind that Griff was siphoning off the choicest items for himself.

However, with Griff absent and Hudson alone in the cockpit, he had started to feel much more at ease. This was despite still being troubled by what

Griff had done, and his part in it, however unwitting. That had been the dangerous and terrifying part of being in space. Now was the beautiful part, Hudson reminded himself, as he piloted the rudimentary, two-man patrol craft towards the Earth-like blue planet. *I may as well enjoy it while I can...* he thought, guessing that his time with the RGF would serve up few good moments like this.

Vivaldi One was one of thirty-nine habitable planets that had been found on the other side of the portals. This was the simple name given to the collection of stable worm holes that had been discovered over a century earlier. Hudson always wondered what must have gone through the minds of the crew that happened upon the very first portal, entirely by accident, all that time ago. He could never remember all of their names, but the name of the captain had always stuck in his mind. *Captain Shaak, like shock...* Hudson mused. *I bet it must have been a shock too...*

Shaak and his crew were hauling gear up from Earth to help build the first moon village, when a guidance malfunction veered them dramatically off course. One moment, they were heading out into deep space, desperately trying to fix the navigational glitch, and the next they had popped through an invisible wormhole. Like a cat pushing through a cosmic cat-flap, they ended up in a new star system, in some distant and unknown part of the galaxy. Even more remarkable was what they found on the other side. The discovery of an Earth-like, habitable, though curiously lifeless planet, would have been startling enough on its own. Yet crashed on the surface was something even more astonishing – the wreckage of an alien spacecraft.

Its discovery was arguably the most significant moment in human history. And it was one that would go on to have profound consequences for civilization. The alien wreck was colossal in scale, like a toppled skyscraper, half-buried in the sandy soil. And though it too was devoid of life, or even any long-decayed evidence of life, it was a goldmine of scientific secrets. Knowledge mined from the alien relics would accelerate Earth's technological expertise by decades in a matter of just a few years.

Shaak's discovery was only the first. Once he and his crew had returned back through the portal to the solar system, the finding was soon made public. The greatest scientific minds on Earth then began to study the wormhole with the principal aim of learning if more existed. Success came two years later when a PhD student in Canada discovered a unique radiation signature. This was later to be named Shaak Radiation, after the unwitting captain who made the first portal discovery.

The name of the PhD student, like the names of Shaak's crew, had long since been forgotten. Hudson doubted that few people today would even know, or care, who Shaak was. All were victims of the passage of time, and the acceptance of wormholes and alien space ships as something that was commonplace, rather than incredible.

The existence of Shaak Radiation pointed the way to further portals. Soon many more were uncovered, not only around Earth, but around the portal worlds too. And through each new portal was found another sterile, habitable world, and another wrecked alien hulk.

The race to unlock the secrets of the alien technology initially led to tense confrontations between the global powers of the time. However, it eventually proved to be a great leveler. It elevated the status of all nations, and solved key issues, like providing cheap, sustainable energy production. Eventually, it spawned the first global united governing body. And as humankind spread to the moon and to new orbital cities, this grew into the Coalition of Earth Territories, or CET.

In the one hundred and twenty years since the discovery of that first portal and alien wreck by Shaak and his crew, the alien technology had made colonization of the solar system possible. It led to the formation of a new faction, split-off from the CET, called the Martian Protectorate, or MP. The Martian Protectorate had since grown to become a super-power in its own right. And unallied to either of these factions was the Union of Outer Portal Worlds, or OPW. This was a union of independent states that had chosen to live on the frontier worlds. All existed beyond the most distant portals – those which were far outside the territories of Mars and Earth.

All told, the discovery of the portals had furthered humankind's reach into the stars by thousands of years in a single century. All of it was made possible because of the tech recovered from inside the labyrinthine guts of the alien hulks. And this was where the relic hunters came in.

In the beginning, the different factions had commissioned private firms to extract the alien secrets from the wrecks. However, corruption and black-market trades led to relics from CET portal worlds being sold for profit in MP territory, and vice versa. Tensions became inflamed and an incident between CET and MP military vessels that left three ships destroyed and fifty dead almost led to an all-out war.

Fortunately, an interplanetary Armageddon was narrowly averted and a summit was convened at the neutral Ceres space station. The objective was to resolve the issue of policing the alien relics, and ensure the fair distribution of tech and wealth. This led to the creation of two new bodies. The relic hunters were licensed privateers who were solely permitted to recover alien relics. And the independent Relic Guardian Force was set up to police the relic hunters and ensure fair play. That had been the theory, in any case. Though as Hudson now knew all too well, it was a far from perfect system. And although the summit had succeeded in preventing war, a bitter resentment still remained between the CET and the Martians. It was like the nuclear-era cold war of the nineteen fifties and sixties, but escalated to an interstellar scale.

Meanwhile, poets and scholars had continued to argue that humanity's reach was exceeding its grasp. Many contended that homo sapiens simply weren't ready to colonize the stars. They argued that while the alien technology had rapidly accelerated humanity's scientific evolution, society had not advanced to nearly the same degree. Far from a fantasy utopia; the malignancies of crime, corruption and sin were still rife on Earth, Mars and throughout all the inhabited portal worlds. And the further from Earth one dared to venture, the more decadent, dangerous and lawless these pockets of human society became.

Eventually, the rate of discovery of new portals slowed, and then stopped altogether. A new portal hadn't been discovered in well over fifty years, and gradually the expeditions to uncover more tailed away. Instead, faction forces and relic hunters chose to focus their efforts on the many discovered worlds and wrecks instead. And, just as the desire to find new portals diminished, so did the interest in learning why they existed in the first place. Few now cared who or what the mysteriously-absent aliens were, where they came from, and why their crashed hulks were found always on sterile worlds. These were now questions that all but the most devoted academics, conspiracy theorists and mystery lovers bothered to ponder over. The wrecks, like the portals, had just become an accepted part of the world people lived in. They were no more fantastical than space travel itself or people living on the moon and Mars.

The significance of the alien wrecks and the relic hunting operations was why, indirectly, Hudson had chosen to join the RGF. Though it was far from his first career choice, or first career.

"Son, I wish you'd do something that you actually gave two shits about," his father had lectured him once. This had been after Hudson had quit yet another gig, that time piloting sub-orbital shuttle taxis across the western United States. "It doesn't matter what it is, just make sure it matters to you, okay?" The problem was, Hudson could never figure out what he cared about, other than flying. It had taken both of his parents to die in a transit accident to galvanize his resolve and sign up to RGF, as a thirty-eight-year-old rookie. *Policing the relic hunting operations that had allowed humans to reach for the stars... that has to be important, right?* Hudson had asked himself. *That has to matter?* So, in the stark absence of anything else to give two shits about, he settled on the RGF. Like a great many of Hudson's decisions, it hadn't panned out quite as he had expected.

The console bleeped, warning him that his entry angle and velocity were off. This was also apparent from the growing vibrations clattering through the hull of the ship. Griff re-emerged from the cargo hold and poked his head into the cockpit.

"Ease up, rook," Griff said, "Landing this thing is the only useful thing you'll do today; you can at least try not to screw that up too." Then he disappeared back into the hold again, no doubt to continue lining his pockets.

Hudson was sure that Chief Inspector Wash, the head of their divisional HQ located on Earth, had assigned Logan Griff as his training officer out of spite. A latecomer to the RGF, Hudson had always seemed to find himself at odds with the core duties of the service. Officially, these were to police the portal worlds and alien crash sites to ensure that the licensed relic hunters all coughed up their share of their finds. The controlling authority took its slice, whether that was the CET, the MP, or the OPW, while the neutral RGF also took a cut to fund its operations. The problem was that the RGF was more corrupt than even the most despicable treasure hunter. This was something Hudson had naively believed to be mere rumor and hearsay before joining up. How wrong he had been.

Hudson checked his dials and readouts and reset the autopilot for atmospheric entry, before arching his neck back to call out to Griff. He considered not doing so, and simply letting the cantankerous beanpole bounce around inside the hold as they buffeted through the atmosphere. However, as much as that would provide him immense satisfaction, he knew Griff would get his own back, only three times worse. As much as it pained him to do so, putting up and shutting up was the best option when it came to Corporal Logan Griff.

"Hey, Griff, you might want to strap in, we're about to punch through the atmosphere," Hudson called out.

There was a short delay, while dull thuds of drawers closing and the chink of metal items clanking together echoed out from the hold. Griff then eventually emerged, cigarette hanging from his bottom lip, looking smug. Hudson could see the pockets of his black, RGF-issue cargo pants were now stuffed full, and he turned back to face his controls, shaking his head.

"Before you get all judgey on me, asshole, that lot back there is probably twenty percent of our quarterly quota," said Griff. He had evidently noticed Hudson's disapproving reaction to his petty pilfering. "I just take a little extra for my trouble, and so should you. The sooner you learn that the better."

"Whatever you say," Hudson answered, trying to come off as nonchalant, but instead sounding condescending.

Griff clicked the harness of his seat into place and then cast his eyes back to the rookie officer in the pilot's chair. His long, wiry eyebrows were pressed together in a sharp vee. "If you hate this job so much, why the hell did you even join the RGF?"

Hudson shrugged, "I thought I would be doing something that mattered."

Griff blew out an obviously faked, mocking laugh, "Making bank is the only damn thing that matters, rook," he said, turning his attention to his own computer console. "You should have done charity work or joined a goddamn monastery."

"Maybe I will," replied Hudson, cheerfully, as flames engulfed the cockpit glass, which steadily polarized to reduce the intensity of the light now flooding inside the normally dark cabin. He didn't want to give Griff the satisfaction of knowing how much his blood was boiling.

"Too late for that," said Griff, as his console chimed an incoming alert. He looked down and read it, before continuing. "You don't get to quit the RGF, not without consequences. That's something else you should have learned before signing up. Like it or not, this is who you are now, so you'd better get used to it. There are far worse ways to spend your time in the RGF than flying a bucket like this."

Hudson sighed, but chose not to answer. There wasn't really any point; Griff's obstinance was as certain as the movement of the planets.

The flames cleared from outside the cockpit and Hudson dove the nimble patrol craft below the cloud line, revealing a lush, yellow-green forest. It would have expanded out beyond the horizon for hundreds of miles, like a vast unbroken sea of leaves, were it not for two features that crudely ruined the otherwise unblemished landscape.

The first was the vast alien wreck itself, smashed into the ground. It lay at the end of a mile-long trench that the titanic vessel had carved into the planet's surface during its final minutes. Set up all around the alien ship was the RGF checkpoint district. This was the border through which all the relic hunters had to pass and declare their finds, or 'scores' as they were known in relic hunter slang.

The second was the mini metropolis and spaceport that had evolved around the wreck, built in a deforested section about four miles square. Colorfully named 'scavenger towns', these settlements serviced the needs of the relic hunters and RGF personnel that were assigned to every portal world. However, in the decades since their foundation, many had become home to thousands more. They were havens for those who preferred life outside the confines of the stricter and more prudish core planets.

Both the scavenger town and the wreck were ugly, alien additions to the world below. And as Hudson watched them both draw closer, he couldn't help feeling that they were like pus-filled sores, festering on otherwise pristine, perfect skin. And considering Vivaldi One was a relatively luxurious inner portal world, that was saying something.

Despite being one of the larger and more developed scavenger towns, Vivaldi One still contained all manner of seedy establishments, curiosity stores and ways to both entertain and get yourself killed. It resembled a large-scale military forward operating base and airfield. Except that outside of the razor-wired camps of the RGF and the CET, it was a debauched and near-lawless place where almost anything goes. Hudson had visited many of these scavenger towns, even before joining the RGF, and he knew Vivaldi One well. Nevertheless, compared to some of the towns on the Outer Portal World planets, it was practically a nunnery.

Hudson flipped the switch to open a comm channel and spoke into his headset microphone. "Vivaldi One, this is RGF patrol craft Scimitar, requesting permission to land..."

The reply was almost instantaneous, but when Hudson heard the voice on the other end of the line, his mood sank even lower than Vivaldi One's setting orange sun. It was the only person in the galaxy he disliked more than Griff – Chief Inspector Jane Wash.

"Patrol Craft Scimitar, permission granted. I'm eager to hear your report, Officer Powell..." said Wash, in a tone that was as sinister as it was threatening.

Great, what the hell is she doing here? Hudson asked himself, rhetorically. Then he caught Griff leering at him out of the corner of his eye. He waited for Hudson to take the hint and meet his gaze fully, before slapping the bulging thigh pockets of his cargo pants.

"Well, at least one of us has made his personal quota this week!" he boasted, and then the sound of the cockpit was once again filled with a cruel, nasal laugh. Griff then drew deeply on his cigarette, before blowing out a thick plume of smoke. "How about you, rook? How are your numbers looking?"

Hudson ignored the question and Griff's smug, sanctimonious face, and focused ahead. His knuckles were white against the bare metal of the control column, and his face burned red hot. He didn't care about consequences, he told himself. He had to find a way out of the RGF, before it drove him to murder.

CHAPTER 3

The sharp clack of Inspector Wash's boot heels on the clinically-white tile floor was all it took to snap the briefing room to attention. As she reached the podium and turned sharply to face her squad, Wash's eyes fell immediately on Hudson, sitting at the front of the room. The look on her face could have turned milk sour.

"So far the Vivaldi portal worlds are running at one hundred and ten percent of quota," Wash began, her voice as sharp as the sound of her heels. She paused and her eyes surveyed the faces of the officers in the room. Hudson knew this was a test to see if anyone would be foolish enough to make any sound that suggested happiness or satisfaction at her announcement. Hudson, naturally, had made such a mistake during his first week on the job. He quickly learned that no matter what percentage over quota her squads were, it was never enough for Wash. "You need to do better!" she eventually screeched, to the surprise of no-one in the room.

Wash then turned her slender frame side-on and pointed a clicker at the back wall. The projected image of the RGF logo then switched to show a still from the gun camera of a patrol craft. Hudson immediately knew what was coming next.

"Now for today's lesson on how to screw up, courtesy of our evergreen rook on the front row, Officer Hudson Powell." Wash delivered the line with uncharacteristic brio. Ridiculing Hudson in front of the squad was a sport she relished, and it was one she never failed to pursue during her sporadic visits to the department stations at the scavenger towns.

To begin with, Hudson thought her visits to simply be a sign of diligence and a zeal for the job. However, it had quickly become apparent that Wash's true motivations were more sordid. In addition to being as crooked as a boomerang, Wash was also a connoisseur of each scavenger town's more underground pleasures. And the scavenger towns were rife with forms of entertainment that could not be found on the more morally-conservative cities on Earth, the moon and Mars.

Wash pressed a button on the clicker and the video began to play. It was a recording of Hudson and Griff's earlier engagement with the rogue relic hunter. Wash commented over the top of the recording, like a sports pundit, which drew frequent smatterings of subdued titters from the room. Then the video reached the point where the relic hunter ship had spun itself around to face them, nose-to-nose. Hudson closed his eyes and waited for the inevitable punchline, as Wash hit the clicker and turned up the audio.

"Wait, what's it doing?"

"It's going to attack, you moron!"

"But relic hunter vessels aren't allowed to carry weapons!"

Precisely on cue, there was a ripple of cruel laughter from the room. Even amongst this ugly melee of snorts and guffaws, Hudson could still clearly pick out Logan Griff's nasal contribution. Wash turned to face the room and then peered down at Hudson, with her lips curving into a thin smile.

"But relic hunter vessels aren't allowed to carry weapons!" Wash repeated, doing a bad impression of Hudson. It sounded even more shrill than her usual, piercing tones. The sycophants in the room obliged with another ripple of laughter. "If it wasn't for the fact we need pilots like you, Officer Powell, I'd scrub your worthless ass from this squad in a heartbeat," Wash added, bitterly. "As it is, it looks like we're stuck with you, for now."

"That's good news, I'd hate to miss out on these inspiring pep talks in the future," said Hudson, with a straight-faced coolness. He actually heard the sharp intake of breath from the officer next to him after he'd finished delivering the line. Hudson knew the smart thing would have been to just shut his mouth, and take Wash's reprimand, but he was tired of being the butt of everyone's jokes.

The crooked smile on Wash's face vanished faster than chips at one of the scavenger town's bent casinos. "What do you think your personal quota is this week, Officer Powell?" Wash asked. Her tone was no longer mocking; this was the chief inspector at her most spiteful.

"I don't know, Chief Inspector Wash," replied Hudson, managing to sound calm and respectful, despite his face feeling like it was melting. "I'd estimate perhaps eighty, eighty-five percent?"

"Try sixty-five percent, Officer Powell," Wash corrected him. The anger and disappointment oozed out of her like blood from a needle prick. "And you'd better get that to at least one hundred, Officer Powell, or your next patrol will be on the walls around the sewage recycler." The room maintained a deathly silence. Wash's squad was well trained, at least in terms of knowing when to laugh, and when to shut the hell up. Hudson played along – he'd pushed his luck to the limit as it was.

Wash sniffed loudly and then rubbed her nose, which was a slightly hotter pinkish color compared to the rest of her face. Hudson observed that it was also slightly swollen. This was no doubt a side-effect of a recent narcotic extravagance that Wash had enjoyed while in the town. She then hit the button on the clicker again, and turned to face the wall, which now showed a list of the squad's next assignments.

Hudson scanned the list, while Wash began to read off the assignments, one-by-one. He raced ahead until he found his name, alongside that of Corporal Logan Griff. He looked along the row and saw his assigned portal world – Brahms Three. *Great...* he thought to himself, *trust Wash to assign me to an even bigger dump than this place...*

Brahms Three was another CET portal world, but it was on the fringe between CET territory and the Outer Portal World planets. Compared to Vivaldi One, the alien wreck on Brahms Three was still relatively unexploited. This meant that it attracted a higher caliber of relic hunter, and generally more trouble. In addition to these more shrewd and ruthless hunters, Brahms Three was also frequented by pirates and mercenaries. These flew in from various grotty OPW outposts to sell their ill-gotten gains, as well as to enjoy the scavenger town's delights.

On the scale of 'beautiful and exciting' to 'dangerous and terrifying', Brahms Three was far towards the latter end of the spectrum. This didn't especially bother Hudson – he'd flown light freighters in and out of Brahms Three for years, prior to joining the RGF. However, its less tightly regulated status simply afforded Griff more opportunity to dip his bony fingers into the cookie jar.

The scavenger town on Brahms Three was also especially vile. It was a gateway between the more regulated CET inner portal worlds and the OPW planets, where almost anything was trafficked, even including people. Of all the assignments on the board it was the worst. This was no doubt why Wash had given it to him; a fact Griff would not let him forget.

Hudson tuned back into the strident tones of Wash as she finished up the briefing. "You all have your assigned duties, now get to them," she hollered, so loud that it hurt Hudson's ears. "I expect to see a marked improvement in claims so that we can close out this week on a high. Get what's due, and anything else you can. Is that clear?"

There was a chorus of, "yes sir!" from the squad, though Hudson didn't join in.

"And for those currently behind, such as Officer Screw Up, here," Wash added, flicking her gaze down to Hudson as she said it, "know that any short-fall will be taken out of your pay." Then she elevated her voice to add emphasis, "Yours *and* your partner's pay..."

Hudson felt a sharp stinging sensation on the back of his neck, and he arched around to see Griff glowering at him. On the floor behind his chair was a half-chewed ball-point pen. Hudson rubbed his neck, and a blob of ink wiped off onto his fingers. It was like being back at school.

"Dismissed!" yelled Wash. There was a sudden screech of chairs against the polished tile floor, as everyone bolted upright, like trained animals. It sounded like the alarm call of a flock of blackbirds. Hudson, however, remained seated.

Griff pushed his way through the throng towards Hudson and bent down to pick up the mangled ball-point pen. He then jabbed the gnawed end into Hudson's chest. "You'd better step up, rook," Griff snarled, peering down at him with his bloodshot eyes. "Because if it comes down to losing my share of the cut, or losing you, I won't hesitate."

Hudson could have grabbed the pen and shoved it into his beady, brown eyes, but he managed to hold his cool. He took the ball-point between his finger and thumb and eased it away from his body, all the while maintaining eye contact with Griff. "You'll get what's due to you, Griff. Of that, I'm certain."

CHAPTER 4

Hudson powered down the engines of the patrol craft and ran through the post-flight checklist. He also hurriedly opened the rear cargo hatch. The idea was to circulate some fresh air into the cabin, to wash away the stench of Griff's farts. Unfortunately, the smell inside the ship was merely replaced by the even more unpleasant stench of Brahms Three's scavenger town.

The distinctive odor was instantly recognizable to Hudson, despite him not having set foot on the planet for several years. Brahms Three was a hot and humid tropical world, which helped to cook up a unique environment. It was a heady mix of street food, fossil-fuel pollution from the cheap ground and air transports, and spicy incense from the seedier bars and nightclubs. The latter was simply to mask the smell of illegal substances, though this never worked. It all combined to create a pungent, sticky mess. Hudson rubbed his thumb and forefinger together and could already feel the fine grit attaching to his skin. Worse still, he knew that the smell would linger on his clothes for days after departing the planet, no matter how vigorously he washed them.

"Hey, rook," called Griff, who had previously gone aft to gather up his personal belongings. "Register our arrival; I'm heading off to check out the town. And remember, we're on duty at second sunrise, local time; don't be late."

Hudson turned to acknowledge Griff, but he was already half-way down the cargo ramp. "Yes, sir..." he said out loud, "I hope you don't catch anything nasty and die horribly..." Then he unclipped his harness, which retracted neatly into the seat back, and stretched out his arms, as if he'd just woken from a restful slumber. Though, in reality, his journey had been long and uncomfortable, made worse by the company. The release of pressure across his chest was welcome, but it also reminded him of how tired he was. He rubbed the bridge of his nose with his thumb and forefinger, and again felt the moist, gritty air of the scavenger town against his skin. "Welcome to paradise..." Hudson muttered to himself as he stood up, his legs feeling like sacks of oats. "Another glorious day in the RGF..."

The journey to Brahms Three had required four portal transitions and had taken over sixteen hours. The farting carcass of Logan Griff had slept for ten of these hours, and been entirely unhelpful for all sixteen. Reaching Brahms was still quicker than traveling to a Martian Protectorate territory. However, the requirement to run through portal checkpoint procedures meant there was relatively little time to relax in-between transitions. If you were lucky to travel when the distance between Earth and Mars was relatively short, and were happy to sustain a little more than one-g, it was possible to sleep for a good part of the journey to MP territory. All Hudson wanted to do now was sleep. Sadly, he had a feeling that Brahms Three would offer him little opportunity for rest.

Hudson secured the cockpit and headed into the rear compartment, grabbing his bag en-route. He then stepped down the cargo ramp into the wall of sticky heat outside. The scavenger town was only a hundred meters beyond the razor-wired border fence of the small RGF airbase. The flickering neon light tubes and thump, thump, thump of the nightclub sound systems were already threatening to give him a headache. He logged their arrival at the docking checkpoint computer and then headed into the main RGF complex. This was nothing more than a hodge-podge collection of crudely interconnected shipping containers. They had been left over from when the base was established, twenty years earlier. It was supposed to have been a temporary structure, but budget cuts and the sheer distance from Earth meant Brahms Three had to make do with what it had.

"Officer Hudson Powell, checking in," Hudson said to the sergeant behind the makeshift main desk. He had tried to sound enthusiastic, but failed miserably. The sergeant was a stout, rough-shaven man in his early sixties. He was slouched over the desk, reading the latest news on an epaper.

"Corporal Griff checked you in already, Officer Hudson Powell," the Sergeant said, without looking up from the epaper. Hudson peered over and saw that he was actually turned to the celebrity gossip section. "You're in luck; you get your own room," he added, casually slinging a key card across the desk. Hudson just caught it before it slid onto the filthy floor. "Strangely enough, we don't get many officers staying here."

"That's the first bit of good news I've had in a while, thanks," said Hudson, holding the key card as if it were a winning lottery ticket. Sixteen hours cooped up with Griff's snoring and farting was about as much as his sanity could take.

"You haven't seen the room yet," said the Sergeant, a wry smile curling his hairy top lip. Though he still hadn't looked up from the epaper. "Crew quarters are just down the main hall and off to the right."

"Where's the canteen?" asked Hudson. In addition to being dog tired, he was also starving.

"Kitchen's closed," answered the Sergeant, "A whole army of damn rodents came in with the last supply shipment. Rat shit all over the place. You'll have to go into the town, not that any of the eateries out there are any cleaner."

"Right," said Hudson, closing his eyes and trying to stay calm, "good to know."

"Good hunting, Officer Hudson Powell," said the Sergeant, with a dismissive waft of his hand. He then returned to his epaper and swiped across to the next section of salacious gossip.

Hudson shifted his pack further up onto his shoulder and set off into the complex. The whole place was as hot as a sauna and stank of stale sweat and mildew. He found his room – number 101, which even in his foul mood managed to elicit a slight chuckle – and pressed the key card to the lock. The door swung open to reveal a space that looked more like a prison cell. There was a narrow single bed, a single storage locker and a small basin. Overall, there was barely enough space to swing one of the base's new rodent inhabitants. Hudson sighed, slung his pack onto the bed, which barely made a dent in the rock-hard mattress, and turned on the faucet. A gurgling noise belched down the spout for several seconds, until a lukewarm, brownish-yellow liquid started to flow out.

"To hell with this, already," Hudson said, staring at himself in the mirror. "I need a drink."

He grabbed his key card and left the room, yanking the door closed behind him. A fat brown rat scurried past along the corridor, seemingly untroubled by Hudson's presence. "Maybe he knows a good place to drink..." Hudson muttered to himself. He then followed the rodent until he found a sign that said, 'To The Scavenger Town'.

CHAPTER 5

Walking through the streets of the scavenger town on Brahms Three was the last place Hudson expected to find himself that night. It was also the last place he wanted to be, besides in a cockpit with Griff. The night air was hot, musky and oppressive, and he was exhausted. However, he desperately needed a drink, and knew exactly where to get one. Though, from memory, the liquor in question was probably as likely to kill him as the vile liquid that had spluttered from the faucet in his prison-cell room.

Hudson meandered along the main boulevard, which was lined on either side by an eclectic assortment of night-time establishments. Like the RGF compound, these were built from converted shipping containers, stacked two or three high. Hudson wasn't interested in any of these illicit businesses, though. He was keeping a suspicious eye on everyone else out for a promenade that night, to avoid getting mugged or pickpocketed. Even so, before he'd even reached the first crossroads, Hudson counted that he'd been offered three different kinds of sex, five different varieties of narcotic, and four invitations out for a fight. For Brahms Three, that still counted as a pretty quiet night.

Despite not having visited the town for over three years, nothing much had changed, Hudson mused. He noticed a few boarded-up bars and nightclubs, alongside several new ones that had probably stolen their trade. Nevertheless, he still recognized all of the places to avoid. This included the scant number of establishments where RGF officers were tolerated. Though, as with most portal worlds, those wearing the RGF uniform were never outright welcomed.

He reached the door of his intended venue, which was themed as a classic twentieth century American-style dive bar. It was called 'The Landing Strip' which, contrary to its suggestive title, wasn't actually a strip club. This was a frequent cause of disappointment for most of the passing trade who entered through its doors. As such, it was more of a haunt for locals, or those, like Hudson, who knew the owner. She was a straight-talking, but generally good-humored retired relic hunter called Martina, or Ma for short. She didn't stand for any nonsense, or for any of the more sordid services provided by other bars and clubs on the boulevard. Consequently, Hudson could pretty much guarantee that Griff wouldn't be in there to ruin his chances of enjoying a quiet drink.

He pushed through the door and the sound of the jukebox playing late twentieth century rock music filled his ears. There were about a dozen other people in the bar, but none of them looked up to see who had entered, and Hudson didn't hang around long enough to give them any reason to. He stepped further inside the bar, his RGF-issue boots thudding resonantly on the solid wooden floor, and slid onto a stool at the bar.

"Well, I'll be damned... If it isn't Hudson Powell," said Ma, who was the only person who had looked up to see who'd entered. She poured a top-up for a woman wearing on over-sized, dark tan leather jacket, and then shuffled across towards Hudson. There was an awkward pause, where Hudson wasn't sure if Ma was going to punch him or kiss him. It made him wonder if he'd forgotten to pay his tab the last time he'd been there. Then Ma reached over the counter and pulled him into an uncomfortable embrace. "How long has it been? A year? Two years?" she added, finally releasing him.

Hudson stretched his neck, trying to iron out the crease that Ma had just added. Her years spent as a relic hunter, climbing around inside alien space ships and fighting off competitors had tempered her into a formidable physical presence, and retirement had done nothing to lessen her athletic stature. If she hadn't been a relic hunter, Ma would have made an epic cage fighter, Hudson had always thought. "A little over three, I think," he answered, rubbing his shoulder.

"That long?" said Ma, appearing genuinely shocked. "Well, I'm glad you're back. I miss your kind around here. Most of the losers who wind up at Brahms Three these days are more crooked than an RGF cop." Then she noticed the uniform that Hudson was wearing, did a double take, and recoiled from him. "What the hell, Hudson, are you a clobber now?"

Hudson scowled, "A what?"

"A clobber," Ma repeated, as if saying it again would make him understand. "Clobber! Claim Robber. An RGF cop, for crying out loud!"

This time the other patrons of the bar did look up. Hudson felt suddenly vulnerable, as if twelve laser sights had just landed on his back. He shifted uncomfortably on his stool, glancing into the room, before looking back at Ma. He noticed that the woman in the leather jacket was also now watching him, while trying not to make it obvious. Hudson met her eyes, and she immediately looked down at her drink. She then smoothed a lock of hair behind her ear, before toying with her whiskey glass, which was empty again.

44

"I haven't heard them called that before," admitted Hudson, turning back to Ma, "but from what I've experienced of the RGF so far, it's not a bad description."

"Then why the hell did you join them?" asked Ma, cocking her head to the side and looking at him, expectantly. "You must have known what you were getting into?"

"Well, no, not really." Hudson was starting to feel and sound defensive. "I mean, I'd heard stories, but I didn't read much into them. You know how people exaggerate, right?"

"Not about the RGF they don't," replied Ma, bluntly. "If anything, people underestimate just how shady a bunch of assholes they all are." Then she held up her hands in a conciliatory gesture. "Sorry..."

Hudson frowned, "Well, I didn't know, okay? I thought policing the alien wrecks would be something worthwhile. You know, something better than just hopping from one dead-end piloting job to another?"

"I take it you're having second thoughts then?" said Ma, rocking back and bringing up two glasses from underneath the counter. She then grabbed a square bottle of whiskey, with no label on the side, from the shelf behind her and poured a long measure into each glass.

Hudson met the bartender's eyes and then downed the shot. It had a kick harder than a champion Thai Boxer, and as it burned its way down the back of Hudson's throat, he couldn't help but let out an apologetic cough.

Ma laughed, "You've gone soft, Hudson Powell. There was a time when a shot of the good stuff wouldn't even cause you to blink."

"Are you sure that's the good stuff?" croaked Hudson, thumping his chest. Ma laughed again, before necking her own shot as easily as if it were water and then refilling both glasses. Unseen by them both, the woman in the leather jacket at the other side of the bar smiled too.

"I always thought you'd make a good relic hunter," Ma went on, this time sipping the amber liquid from her glass. "You're a great pilot, and you've always struck me as an honest, dependable kind of guy. Those traits are hard to come by in a partner."

Hudson also took a sip of the whiskey, which didn't burn quite so badly this time. This was likely on account of the numbing of his mouth and throat from the last shot. "It certainly has some appeal, I can't deny that," he conceded. Then his father's voice echoed in his ears again, telling him to do something that mattered, and he sighed. "It's just that I always thought relic hunting was a bit..." He stopped, realizing he was about to talk himself into a corner.

"Go on..." said Ma, raising her carefully tweezered eyebrows a little.

"Well, I suppose a bit, you know, disreputable."

Ma's laugh blared out into the bar, drowning out the jukebox and causing one or two of the clientele to shout out at her to be quiet. Ma fired a few blue expletives back at them and then finished her whiskey, before pouring another and topping up Hudson's half-empty glass. "You waltz in here, wearing a damn clobber's uniform, and call us scavengers 'disreputable'?" she said, wiping a tear from her eye. "You may be honest, Hudson Powell, but you're none too bright."

Hudson had already been mocked enough by Griff and Chief Inspector Wash over the last few months. Ma calling his intelligence into question was different, and much harder to stomach. He didn't care what Griff or Wash thought of him, but Ma was someone he respected and looked up to. Coming from Ma, it actually hurt.

"Damn it, Ma, I'm not an idiot," Hudson snapped. "I had some personal stuff to deal with, and I wanted to make good on a promise, that's all." Ma was silent; like any good bartender, she knew when to speak and when to listen. "I honestly thought putting on this uniform and policing the wrecks would matter. I wanted to do something important." He looked down at the hardwood bar, decorated with dozens of overlapping, ring-shaped stains from the bottoms of whiskey glasses. He idly wondered how many other troubled drinkers had once sat where he had, and then necked the shot. It went down easier than the first, but still involuntarily forced him to squint one eye shut.

Ma seemed to realize that she had tickled a nerve, and her tone softened a little. "Clothes don't make a man," she said, grabbing a ragged cloth and mopping the bar, where she'd spilled some of the whiskey. "Or a woman for that matter. But I'll tell you this for nothing; you won't find what you're looking for wearing that uniform."

"Doesn't matter now anyway," replied Hudson, as Ma topped up his glass again. He was filled with the warm fuzzy sensation that came from drinking strong liquor too quickly, and it had also helped loosen his tongue. "As much as I want to, you don't get to just quit RGF. Basically, I'm screwed."

There was a shout from one of the other patrons at the far end of the bar. Ma answered it with another expletive, before she ducked down under the counter and returned with a bottle of beer, covered with a light frosting of ice. She slid the neck down sharply across the counter, popping off the metal cap with a satisfying fizz, and then placed it in front of Hudson.

"This one's on the house," she said, before yelling again at the impatient punter and strutting towards him.

Hudson took a swig of the beer, which felt blissful, like jumping into a cool shower after a hot sauna. He then glanced along the bar to see where

Ma had got too. Instead, he caught the eye of the woman in the leather jacket that was too big for her. In his warm and fuzzy-headed state, Hudson decided to smile and shoot up a conversation.

"Don't worry, I'm not here to arrest you," he began, believing it to be a witty and charming opening. The woman just looked away sharply and concentrated on her whiskey glass instead, which was empty. Realizing that his joke was perhaps not as funny as he'd thought, given the RGF's reputation, he tried again. "Hey, sorry, bad joke. For what it's worth, I think I probably dislike the people who wear this uniform far more than you do."

The woman glanced across, half-smiled at him, and then started to play with the empty glass, running her finger around the rim. Encouraged, Hudson tried again to engage with her. He wasn't trying to hit on her; he was just happy-drunk and feeling chatty. Though now that he looked more closely, the woman was certainly pretty, in a mysterious, grungy kind of way. "How's the hunt going. Made your fortune yet?"

"If I had then I'm sure you RGF assholes would only try to take it away from me," the woman replied, huffily. She was still playing with the rim of the glass.

"Not me, I'm one of the good bad guys," Hudson replied, before taking another swig of beer. He was unwilling to let this stranger darken his inebriated high spirits.

The woman pushed back the stool, which screeched across the floor like someone drawing their fingernails across a blackboard. She tossed a few hardbucks on the bar, before heading for the door. She stopped alongside Hudson and shot him a sideways glance. "I'm afraid I didn't score this time. And you're not going to score either, hotshot. Enjoy your beer."

There was a cackle of laughter from the regulars, followed by the more familiar chuckle of Ma. The hunter-turned-barkeep then moved over to pick up the money and clear away the woman's glass. "Nice try, Hudson Powell. Seems that not everyone likes a man in uniform..."

However, Hudson wasn't paying attention to Ma's friendly jibe. As the woman had got up to leave, her leather jacket had briefly swayed open. It was only for a second, but it was enough for an object tucked into an inside pocket to catch Hudson's eye. It had a metallic luster, and was rough-cut, like a shard of crystal, but it also reflected and refracted the light in the bar in a way he'd never seen before. In fact, the best description Hudson could think of was that it looked 'alien'.

Hudson sat back and set his inebriated mind to the task of analyzing what it could be, and why she was carrying it with her. If it was a relic she already owned, perhaps from a previous score, then it would be foolish to carry it around. This was especially the case at night, in a town as dangerous as Brahms Three. Relic hunters were hardly averse to risk, but most were smart enough to be paranoid. And a smart hunter would keep their valuable finds safely locked away from potential thieves, or disreputable fellow hunters.

The alternative was that she had scored it from the alien wreck on Brahms Three. However, if that were true then it should have been locked up in the claims vault, ready for auction or transfer to her ship, not tucked inside her jacket pocket. Hudson may not have been an RGF cop for long, but he knew enough to spot a smuggler. His hunch was that this woman was gearing up to run a unique new artefact off world, without paying taxes to the CET and the RGF.

"What's her story?" Hudson asked Ma, while twirling the neck of the bottle between his thumb and forefinger.

"I guess she just doesn't like you," said Ma, with a smirk.

Hudson rolled his eyes, "I mean it Ma, there's something about her that's... off. And I don't just mean that my charms didn't work on her."

Ma moved back in front of Hudson and picked up the whiskey that she'd left there earlier. "She's been coming here for a couple of days, but doesn't say that much," said Ma, with a nonchalant shrug of her toned shoulder muscles. "If I recall, her ship is pretty beat up. Some crappy old lease from a shipyard in Hunter's Point, from what I gathered."

Hudson snorted a laugh, "Hunter's Point? That's where I'm from. Bayview, I mean, born and bred."

"Seems that it's written in the stars for you two then..." said Ma, wickedly.

Hudson shook his head and took another swig of the beer. Ma filled the silence with the remainder of what she knew about the mysterious woman.

"All I remember is that she talked about needing a big score to pay off some debts at home. Has a family there, I gathered," Ma went on, sipping the whiskey again. "But she's out here alone, and Brahms Three is no place to go hunting solo. I told her she should stick to the safer near-Earth portal worlds, but she seemed pretty determined. Can't say I blame her; it's hard to bag a decent score from the near-Earth wrecks now. Hunters have mostly picked them clean."

As Ma was talking, three men got out of their chairs from the back corner of the room and quickly walked to the door. None of them spoke, or acknowledged Ma when she called out to thank them. Hudson looked at their table and saw three beer glasses, all still about three-quarters full. He scowled and wrinkled his nose, before turning back to Ma. "Who were those guys?"

"Never seen them before," said Ma, with another shrug. "Came in just after the girl did." Then she snapped her fingers, "Ericka, that's her name. I knew I knew it."

Hudson had a bad feeling in his gut, and he was sure it wasn't just from the combination of whiskey and beer. Either way, his instincts told him something was up, and that he had to follow. "I'll catch you later, Ma, thanks for the drinks."

"Hey, the beer is on the house, the whiskey is on you," replied Ma, with an undertone that said pay up quickly, or else.

Hudson smiled, "Fine, pass me the credit scanner."

"Hardbucks only, mister," said Ma, rubbing her finger and thumb together.

"Seriously?" said Hudson, patting himself down. Hardbucks was the more colloquial name given to physical currency, which was almost entirely phased out back on Earth. He knew he had some hardbucks on him somewhere and eventually found a few notes, scrunched up in the bottom of his back pocket. He dropped a mangled hundred on the bar and said, "Here, keep the change."

Ma grabbed the note and stuffed it into her skinny jeans. Hudson then slipped off the stool – almost literally because of the huge amount of alcohol he'd imbibed – and hurried to the door.

"I hope you get lucky, Hudson Powell!" Ma called out to him, as the door swung shut. Hudson didn't answer, and just ran out into the night. He was following a hunch, and most likely also following trouble.

CHAPTER 6

Hudson nearly gave himself whiplash as he twisted his head from side to side, peering down the side-streets outside the Landing Strip. There was no sight of Ericka, or the three men that he suspected had followed her out into the night. Instead, there was just the usual assortment of drunks, night workers and street workers. They were all either minding their own business or soliciting for some.

Which way, damn it? Hudson asked himself. He was now regretting the numerous shots of whiskey, which had turned his brains to mush. *Think, damn it, think...* he urged himself, *where would she be going?* He doubted Ericka would be headed to another bar, unless his company and jokes really had been that bad. The alternative was back to her hotel or hostel. "She's strapped for cash, so a hotel is unlikely, which leaves the main hostel," Hudson reasoned, "but where the hell is it?" He squeezed his eyes shut and tried to remember how the scavenger town was laid out, picturing it in his mind like a map. Slowly the alcohol-induced fuzz resolved, and he recalled the layout more clearly, but he still couldn't picture the hostel.

"You know, talking to yourself is a sign of madness," came a voice from behind him. It was Ma, resting against the doorframe. She pulled a thin cigar out of the front pocket of her skinny jeans and placed it in her mouth, before lighting it with an ancient Harley Davidson zippo.

"Ma, the hostel! How do I get to the hostel?!" Hudson blurted out. He was doing nothing to dispel the perception that he might have gone a little crazy.

"Down the boulevard and right along Heide," said Ma. She pointed to where Hudson needed to go, and then blew a plume of smoke in the same direction.

"Thanks!" said Hudson, immediately setting off at a sprint. The hot night air whistled past his ears, though he still managed to catch Ma calling out, "Be careful, you damn fool!"

Hudson reached the junction between the Boulevard and Heide Street and slid around the corner. He collided with a couple of drunks, who shouted expletives at him, and then picked up the pace again. His legs and lungs burned even hotter than Ma's cigar, but the sudden burst of adrenalin had started to clear his head, and now he was questioning what the hell he was doing. Racing off into the night after a stranger, based solely on a hunch was mad enough. However, his clearer head also reminded him that Heide was one of the streets best avoided, especially at night.

The hostel was about a hundred meters ahead when he passed by a narrow alley and heard glass shattering. Sliding to a stop, he backed up and peered down the alley, which threaded behind a row of bars and clubs. His heart started thumping even harder as he saw the three men, one of whom was already on the floor with blood leaking from his bald head. The woman, Ericka, was there too, holding a short, twisted piece of copper pipe. His hunch had been right, but his sixth sense hadn't prepared him for what to do next. In the absence of any better ideas, Hudson did what he usually did, which was to go with his instincts.

"Hey, what's going on down there?!" Hudson yelled. This immediately grabbed the attention of all three men, including the injured man, who was climbing back to his feet.

"Piss off!" one of them shouted back to him, before turning to face Ericka again.

"RGF, stand down now or I will arrest you!" Hudson called out. He seized his RGF badge from inside his jacket and held it out, as if it had some sort of magical power to subdue criminals. He wished he'd brought his sidearm, even though regulations forbade him to carry it while off duty. *It's not like the RGF gives a shit about following regulations...* Hudson thought. He also didn't know why he imagined identifying himself as RGF would have any effect. Nor did he know how he was going to arrest three belligerent men on his own, especially since he was half-cut and out of breath. Nevertheless, his order certainly did the trick of stopping the muggers in their tracks.

The man who appeared to be the ring-leader turned around and held out his arms, smiling. "Oh, look boys, it's the RGF," he said, mockingly. "We'd better do as he says then, hadn't we?" There was a smattering of laughter from the other two, though neither looked particularly amused. Then the ring-leader lowered his arms and his smile twisted downward. He turned to the bald man and said, "Wilkes, sort out the filthy clobber, while we handle the nice lady here."

The bald man broke off and started to pace towards Hudson, grimacing as if he was chewing a wasp. He reached into the pocket of his cargo pants and pulled out something metallic, which he then proceeded to slip over his fingers.

A knuckle duster? You have got to be kidding me... Hudson thought as the man who had been identified as 'Wilkes' approached, narrowed eyes locked on to his.

He looked about the same height as Hudson, but was carrying perhaps fifty pounds more. He moved with a calm confidence and swagger that suggested he could handle himself. Hudson had dealt with his type before. His many years spent piloting freighters and taxi flyers had given him experience of more than his fair share of cocky troublemakers. Even so, he still hoped he hadn't bitten off more than he could chew.

"Hold it there, I'm warning you!" Hudson yelled, holding a hand out like a traffic cop, but the man just smiled and raised his fist.

"None of your bent buddies are here to help you now, clobber," he said, edging closer to Hudson, fist pulled back, ready to strike. "RGF scumbags have stolen plenty from us in the past, so I'm gonna enjoy getting my money's worth outta you."

Wilkes stepped towards him and threw a swift cross with his armored fist, but Hudson managed to dodge it without trouble. He then blocked a follow up strike from Wilkes' other fist. Either the alcohol was wearing off, or it had dulled his senses just enough that he wasn't overthinking the fight.

Hudson countered by snapping a quick jab of his own into the bald man's nose, which was enough to give him pause. The sound of metal clanking against metal then resonated down the alleyway. Hudson could hear yells and cries of exertion and pain, but he didn't dare take his eyes off Wilkes.

"I didn't steal anything from you," said Hudson, feigning an attack and drawing Wilkes forward. The bald man swung a hard cross that whistled past so close Hudson felt the air rush past his face. However, the miss had also left Wilkes vulnerable. Taking full advantage, Hudson hammered a punch into Wilkes' kidneys, sending the man reeling back into the wall of a rusted shipping container. This was just one of dozens that were stacked high, lining Heide Street all the way down to the hostel. It was one reason why the street was bad news – too many alleys, and not enough ways to escape trouble should it find you, or you find it.

Wilkes roared and rebounded towards Hudson, flashing punches and forcing him to backpedal and defend. The metal of the knuckle duster clipped his shoulder, and Hudson bit down against the pain. Luckily, it was just a glancing blow and not enough to shatter bone.

Adrenalin mixed with fear had combined to clear Hudson's head. Added to this was a powerful surge of anger, caused by being punched with a weapon that belonged in ancient history. Hudson was suddenly filled with resolve. All the frustration of the last few weeks – the constant jibes by Griff and the mocking, condescension from Wash – suddenly poured out of him like a pan boiling over. He grabbed the lapels of Wilkes' thin cotton jacket and charged him back against the container wall. The bald man slammed into the metal with such force that it felt like the entire stack wobbled from the impact. Wilkes lashed out again, but Hudson blocked the blow and then drove his forearm into Wilkes' nose. It connected sweetly, making a hollow crunching sound. Wilkes barely had time to process the sensation before Hudson had driven a knee sharply up into the man's groin. It was a move no less vulgar than his adversary's employment of a brass knuckle, but it was just as effective. Wilkes dropped to the ground faster than a broken elevator.

Hudson sucked in gulps of air, again tasting the incense-tainted decadence of the scavenger town in each labored gasp, and then looked back toward the alley. The second of the remaining two men was down, this time seemingly for good. However, the ring leader was still standing, and now he had a knife aimed at Ericka's throat. She was bleeding from a cut above her eye, but she didn't look scared; she looked as fierce as Hudson felt, and Hudson was furious. The RGF may not have cared about ripping people off, but Hudson Powell did, and he wasn't going to let this gang of thugs get away with it. It didn't matter who they were robbing; this wasn't about Ericka, or any macho notion of riding to the rescue of a damsel in distress. He was just done with letting crooked assholes do what they wanted and get away with it.

He reached down and stripped the knuckle duster from his unconscious former foe's fingers and slid it onto his right hand. Sucking in another lungful of humid air, he then set off towards the alley. The whiskey was still lending him some courage, though he was clear-headed enough to know that what he was doing was pretty stupid. However, as others had a habit of reminding him, Hudson had a tendency to make dumb choices. The difference was, this time he no longer cared. If being smart meant walking away when someone was in trouble, or stealing from someone just to make a quota, then he'd rather be a fool. He just hoped he wouldn't end up a dead one.

CHAPTER 7

The last remaining attacker teased the tip of the blade against Ericka's neck, and watched as Hudson approached. Hudson measured his steps carefully, not taking his eyes off the man for a second.

"Walk away, clobber, or I'll slit the nice lady's throat," threatened the man. "This has nothing to do with the RGF. You'll get your cut, regardless, but she'll get a bigger cut if you don't piss off."

Hudson clenched his fist, feeling the metal bite into the folds between his knuckles, and then glanced across to Ericka. She still looked calm, remarkably so considering the blade had now nicked her skin. This had caused a trickle of blood to flow down her neck. Her eyes met his and then flicked down, like a snake's tongue, before she looked back at her attacker, who hadn't seen the subtle exchange. Hudson quickly scanned his eyes down her body and saw that Ericka was wearing what looked like a stun ring on her left hand. It was essentially a small electroshock buzzer. It looked like a common piece of jewelry, but pressed against a particularly sensitive part of the body, it gave enough of a belt to stun an ox.

Hudson held up his hands and took a half-step forward. He knew what Ericka was suggesting, and knew what he had to do. Although, like his other recent choices, it ranked pretty high on the 'dumb' scale.

"Look, let's do a deal," said Hudson, locking eyes on the man. "Ditch your two goons, and we'll split the profits between us. Then, at the checkpoint, I'll 'overlook' your contribution to the RGF. That way, we both win."

The man laughed, "You must think I'm an idiot," he said, eyes moving to Hudson and then back to Ericka. The blade was still pressed against the relic hunter's skin. "You'll just stiff me for another cut at the checkpoint. You RGF are all the same. And now all you're doing is killing her." The tip of the blade dug a little deeper into Ericka's flesh and she winced, pushing herself flat against the metal container wall in order to release some of the pressure. Despite Hudson's best efforts not to react, he also flinched. His eyes flicked from the trickle of blood on Ericka's neck back to the man.

He could tell the mugger had noticed his discomfort.

"No, I don't think you're like the others," the man said, smiling. "You won't risk getting this nice lady killed. So why don't you just piss off, like a good little clobber?"

Hudson realized he had to change tactics. Time was running out, and this man seemed determined enough to do what he threatened. The mugger had called Hudson's bluff, so now he either had to back down, or go all in. And walking away was something he just couldn't do. Hudson knew what he was about to do was a risk, but he'd run out of time and choices. He just hoped his gamble would work, because if not then he risked getting Ericka – and himself – killed.

"I don't give a shit about her, or you," said Hudson, playing the role expected of him – the villainous, bent RGF cop. "So, go on, kill her then," he continued, "I'll have smashed in your skull before her body hits the ground. Either way, I win. You should know the RGF always wins."

The man's eyes narrowed slightly as he processed Hudson's new threat. Suddenly, he didn't appear so cocky or confident, and in his moment of indecision, his focus, and his knife, slipped away from Ericka's throat. Hudson didn't need to make the first move, because Ericka seized the opportunity to break free. She slid out from beneath the point of the blade before slapping the mugger's hand away.

Without giving the man time to react, Hudson attacked. Time seemed to move in slow motion as his fist pushed through the sticky air, neon lights reflecting off the scuffed metal surface of the knuckle duster. Hudson could see the fear in the man's eyes, but fear hadn't dulled his reactions. Hudson's fist sailed past the mugger's head, clanging into the container wall like a butler ringing a dinner gong. The shock of the impact resonated down his arm and he yelled in pain. Then the knife slashed down towards him, missing his face barely by the thickness of a cat's whisker. Hudson retreated, but he was still vulnerable. The mugger's hand drew back again, ready to thrust the knife into Hudson's chest. He was a mere second away from being stabbed when Ericka rushed forward and jabbed the ring into the mugger's neck. The electroshock device activated and delivered a ten microcoulombs shock. The mugger convulsed grotesquely for a few seconds while Ericka held the ring against his skin, before she drew back and watched as he collapsed in a heap.

Hudson dropped to a crouch, resting back against the container. He blew out a loud sigh, "I was hoping you'd do that..."

Ericka also dropped low, but instead of signaling her relief at making it out of the scrape alive, she grabbed her attacker's blade, and angled it towards Hudson.

"So, what now?" she said, hand shaking slightly, "Are you going to try to rob me too?"

Hudson rose back up slowly, keeping a careful watch on the blade, before meeting Ericka's eyes. "I told you already; I'm not like that. I just had a gut feeling something was up, and followed to make sure you were alright."

"Oh sure, a white knight in a black and blue RGF uniform," said Ericka, dismissively. "I'm not buying that for a second."

Hudson sighed again, this time more out of exasperation than relief, and held up his hands in submission. "Look, believe whatever you like, lady, I've had enough whiskey and excitement for one night."

Hudson dusted himself off, disregarding any threat from the knife being waved at him. He smiled wearily at Ericka, and then trudged back down the alley towards Heide Street.

"You're actually serious?" Ericka called after him. "You really just came out here to help me?"

Hudson stopped and looked back. "Yes, just like I said." Then he pointed at Ericka's leather jacket. "And if you can stand to accept some more help, I'd strongly suggest you declare whatever it is you're trying to smuggle out of here in that jacket." Ericka pulled the jacket tighter across her chest, an obvious tell that Hudson was right about her hiding something. "I may not want to take it from you, but the other RGF cops will. And if you try to run through the checkpoint perimeter, which I guess you're planning to do, they'll shoot you down and claim it as salvage." Ericka didn't answer, but her posture had relaxed and she had lowered the knife. "See you around, Ericka," Hudson added, with a tired salute, before turning and walking away again.

"I don't know what it is..." Ericka called out, again causing Hudson to stop and look around.

"You don't know what what is?" asked Hudson.

Ericka hesitated for a split second and then reached inside her jacket, before removing a short crystal shard. It had the same peculiar mix of metallic luster and glassy shimmer as the item Hudson had caught a glimpse of in the bar. He started walking back towards her, tentatively so as not to appear threatening. It must have taken a lot for Ericka to reveal the object to him. However, despite this unexpected gesture of trust, she was still wound up tighter than an ignition coil.

"I found it on the alien wreck," said Ericka, momentarily mesmerized by the reflections and refractions of the neon lights in the crystal. "I slipped and fell through a hull fracture into a section of the ship that seemed to have been completely unexplored. I made it out with a heap of good stuff, including this. But then these bastards caught up with me before I made it back to the checkpoint district." As she said this, Ericka kicked the legs of the lead mugger that she'd just shocked into unconsciousness. "So, this and a few other relics is all I have left. If I declare the crystal, and it is something previously undiscovered, CET might hold it for analysis. Then it could be weeks or even months before I see a dollar of my claim. And that's assuming the clobbers don't stiff me out of it..." she paused and looked down, "Sorry, force of habit..."

"Don't apologize," said Hudson smiling, "I meant it when I told you I likely hate their guts more than you do."

Ericka met his eyes again, smiling comfortably and at ease for the first time.

"How come they didn't find that too?" asked Hudson, gesturing towards the crystal.

Ericka pulled open her over-sized leather jacket and slipped the crystal back into a hidden pocket. "It's lined with a material that seems to block Shaak radiation," she said, now speaking much more freely. "It's a mix of materials that are all pretty hard to find. I stumbled on the combination by accident, after a checkpoint scanner failed to pick up one of the items from my score. It's only a small pocket, but still helpful for hiding things you don't want found." Then just as quickly as her mood had lightened, she appeared to get swallowed into an abyss of despair. "I need this score," she said, urgently, almost pleading with him. "My brother got hurt at work, lost his job and he can't get another, not all messed up as he is. He's about to get kicked out on the street." She took a step towards Hudson, her eyes now even more imploring. "If that happens, they'll take his kids. They won't give them to a scavenger like me, not that I'd be any good to them, anyway. I sold everything I could just to lease a ship and come out to this shithole planet to find a big score. I've already had most of it stolen from me, but I still have a few decent items hidden away on my ship. And together with whatever this alien crystal thing is, it might just be enough to bail him out." Hudson continued to listen, but he already knew what she was leading up to. "I can't hide everything inside my jacket," Ericka continued. "So, when I do blast out of here, I'm going to trip the sensor barrier and bring a lot of heat down on myself. There's no way in hell my crappy leased ship can outrun an RGF patrol craft."

Hudson had patiently listened to the story, all the while feeling like dirt, because he didn't believe it was true. Rookie RGF cop or not, he wasn't naïve. He'd been around enough to have been fed a sob story or ten before. He knew there was a good chance Ericka was making it all up, just to gain his sympathy and help, but this time he didn't care. True story or fabrication; it didn't matter. All he knew was that he'd rather this woman keep the new alien relic, than allow some asshole like Griff steal it from her.

"You want me to help you get your score off world?" said Hudson, levelly. "You want me to turn a blind eye?"

Ericka took another step towards him, "Whatever is left of the profits, after I bail out my brother, you can keep..."

Hudson waved a hand at her, "I don't want your money."

Ericka frowned, and grabbed her jacket, hugging it tightly around her body. "Then what do you want? You must want something. Everyone wants something, isn't that right, officer..."

"Powell. My name is Hudson Powell," replied Hudson, "And you can forget the officer part; just call me Hudson."

"So, what is it you want, Officer Powell?" asked Ericka, refusing to use Hudson's given name. "You'd risk your job, and even jail, and you don't want a cut?"

"I just want to do the right thing," said Hudson, surprising himself with the answer. Ericka raised a doubtful eyebrow. "Hey, I know it sounds dumb and corny, but that's really all there is to it. I'm supposed to make sure people get their due. So, that's what I'm going to do."

"Fair enough," said Ericka, as the second mugger that she'd knocked out earlier started to rouse. "We should get out of here. I've got a bottle back in my room at the hostel. We can talk more about the plan there, if you like?"

"I think I've had enough to drink for one night," said Hudson, rubbing the back of his neck. Though he couldn't deny the offer was more appealing than heading back to his prison-cell room at the RGF compound.

Ericka took another step forward, tossing the knife to the floor as she did so. "I think I've had enough to drink too. We could just talk?"

Hudson straightened up; Ericka was now so close that he could almost feel her breath on his face. It was a strange but intoxicating mix of whiskey and fruit gum. "I'm afraid I'm not much of a talker either," he added. It felt like the short space between them had just become electrified.

"So, let's not do any talking either..."

CHAPTER 8

Logan Griff was pacing up and down outside the RGF patrol craft when Hudson finally arrived. He was over forty minutes late for their scheduled departure. Griff had the look of someone who'd just stepped in dog muck wearing new shoes. And as Hudson approached, face flushed red and out of breath from running, he wasted no time in launching into an assault.

"Where the hell have you been, rook?" snarled Griff, "I've been here for over an hour, waiting for your pea-green ass to make an appearance."

Hudson severely doubted that Griff had been waiting for that long, but he was in no position to push back. He'd given Griff the perfect excuse to lay into him, and his asshole TO wasn't going to pass up the opportunity.

"Sorry, I... overslept," lied Hudson. The truth was that he had woken in plenty of time to make it back to the RGF compound for their scheduled launch, but events had conspired against him. Specifically, those events were waking up, naked, next to Ericka in her compact single-bed rack in the hostel, and being 'persuaded' by her not to leave. He hadn't really required much persuasion, and Hudson didn't regret his choice even for a nanosecond, despite now being faced with the grim, beanpole-like presence of Griff. His cantankerous training officer could lay into him all he wanted; it was like water off a duck's back.

"I was banging on your door for a good five minutes solid!" Griff yelled.

"What can I say? I'm a heavy sleeper," replied Hudson. He was pushing his luck more than he had any right to, but there was no way even Logan Griff was going to sour his mood. The previous night had been one of the wildest and most exciting of his entire life, and he didn't care about the consequences. In fact, he didn't care about the RGF at all. They could charge him and boot him out for all he cared. And the more he thought about it, the more he realized he almost wanted them to. It would be less messy and controversial than him trying to leave an organization that supposedly no-one ever quit.

The corruption and petty-mindedness of Wash and Griff was pervasive throughout the entire organization. This meant that anyone who turned their back on the RGF could expect constant harassment, wherever they went, for the rest of their life. Yet as much as getting kicked out would be simpler, he also didn't want to give Griff and Wash the satisfaction of having him fired. As such, he'd made up his mind to transmit his resignation the moment Ericka was safely away through the portal, where the RGF could no longer touch her.

"Just get on-board, rook," snapped Griff, shaking his head. "I'm going to write you up and report this incident to Chief Inspector Wash. She can deal with you. With any luck, you'll get booted or assigned to permanent night-watch. Either way, at least I'll finally be rid of you."

"Do what you have to do," said Hudson, cheerfully, "I really don't give a shit."

Of all the responses that Griff might have anticipated, the pained look on his face suggested that this was not one of them. It was as if Griff had just stepped in another pile of crap. Hudson breezed past him and walked up the cargo ramp into the small patrol craft. He realized that in all likelihood this was going to be his last duty shift as an RGF cop. This was assuming Griff responded as explosively as he predicted he would. That fact should have terrified him, but it didn't; it felt liberating. It felt like he was being set free.

All through training, and every moment since graduating, he had refused to believe the horror stories about the RGF. He now realized he'd just been telling himself what he wanted to hear. Even during his training, when he saw glimpses of the corruption he'd been warned about, he still turned a blind eye. He hadn't wanted to admit to himself that he'd made a terrible mistake. He'd never been sure of much in his life, but this he knew with absolute certainty – he had to quit the RGF, no matter what it cost. What came next, he didn't know, but he'd rather face an unknown future than accept the depressing reality of life as a 'clobber'.

He slid down into the pilot's chair and began to run through the pre-flight checklist. He then heard the heavy thump of Griff's size fourteen boots coming up the ramp behind him. *Here we go...* thought Hudson, preparing for the inevitable dressing down.

"I don't believe you'd really make it that easy for me to get rid of you, so what's your game here, rook?" asked Griff. He had moved over next to his chair and was leaning on the backrest. "I know you're dumb, but you're not that dumb."

Hudson didn't look at Griff and just continued to run through the checks. He then powered up the engines and closed the rear cargo ramp. "I wouldn't expect you to understand," Hudson replied, casually, while finishing the last of the procedures. "So just accept it as a parting gift." Then he swiveled his chair to face Griff. "That is what you wanted, right? To finally see the back of me?"

Griff huffed a laugh, "You're up to something."

"Nope," replied Hudson, breezily, though he could see that Griff was now deeply distrustful of his motives.

"Then why report for duty at all?" said Griff, pulling a cigarette and bullet-shaped lighter from a black packet in his breast pocket. He placed the cigarette between his puckered lips, revealing creases all over his gaunt face. He lit the smoke, all the while keeping his eyes focused on Hudson. "There's something you're not telling me," Griff added, before taking a long drag and plucking the cigarette out of his mouth with his bony fingers. Then he jabbed the smoldering stick towards Hudson, spilling ash onto the deck, and blew out the smoke in a plume above his head, like a factory tower. "If you cut some sort of deal with a scavenger crew last night, you won't get away with freezing me out. I'll find out and I'll get my share, whether you like it or not."

Now Hudson laughed, "I thought I was supposed to be a dumb rook? You really think I've struck up some sort of big-time deal in one night?" He swiveled his chair back to face the controls and added, "The truth is that this job sucks and I want out. But until my resignation goes through, I'm going to do my duty. Because, unlike you, I actually care about doing things properly, by the book."

"By the book," laughed Griff, before taking another long drag and blowing it out. "You really believe that crap, huh? Well, whatever you say, rook. If you want to leave, I'll gladly help you out the door." He shook his head in disbelief, then dropped down into his seat and enabled his console. Cigarette ash spilled over the switchgear as he did so. "Get us airborne; the sooner this shift is over, the sooner you can be out of my sight."

Hudson was banking on Griff's desperately low opinion of him to ultimately dispel any further doubts he may have had. However, the truth was Hudson did have a motive for pulling one final shift. That motive was Ericka. He couldn't help her escape if he was already stripped of his duties and unable to fly. He knew there was still a possibility that her sob story about her brother was a lie. If that was true then she'd only invited him to her bed to gain his trust. Deep down he didn't believe that, though, and he didn't care either way. He was going to help her get off world, because he liked her, and he hated the RGF; Griff most of all. Whether Ericka was a scoundrel or not, he'd still rather she kept the alien artefact than allow Griff to line his pockets at her expense.

Hudson radioed the tower and quickly received clearance to take off from a bored-sounding air traffic controller. He increased power to the vertical thrusters and eased the patrol craft into the warm blue sky. When he was clear of the base and scavenger town, he reviewed their orders on his console. Their first port of call was to deliver essential supplies to the RGF guard station on the alien wreck. He checked aft and saw the boxes had already been loaded before his tardy arrival. "Looks like we're doing the sandwich run first," said Hudson, pointing to the boxes.

Griff craned his narrow neck aft, cigarette hanging from his bottom lip, and then flopped back into his seat. "Great, as if today couldn't get any worse."

Hudson shook his head and then swung the nose of the patrol craft out towards the wreck. Already, the great alien hulk dominated the horizon in front of the ship. It lay at rest in the dusty soil like the fossilized remains of a monstrous prehistoric centipede. Hudson was immediately transfixed by its epic size and the beauty of its symmetrical design. Knowing it might be his last chance to see a wreck up close, he stepped harder on the throttle pedal in order to speed up their arrival. Outside of the RGF personnel and registered relic hunters, few others were ever allowed inside the hulks. Hudson had only ever set foot on the outer hull once before. And since this was going to be his last mission before quitting the RGF, he welcomed the chance to get up close. Perhaps he'd even venture inside, while he still could.

Hudson's giddy anticipation was in stark contrast to Griff's reluctant tolerance of their 'sandwich run'. Strangely, for an officer in the Relic Guardian Force, Griff detested being made to visit the alien wrecks, and he considered the task of delivering food and water to the guards stationed there as beneath him. Griff's sole interest in the ancient alien vessels was how much money he could make from them. Specifically, by extorting the relic hunters out of their scores.

"ETA, ten minutes," said Hudson, though Griff just ignored him. He glanced across, noting that Griff had now put his feet up on the console and was resting back with his eyes closed. The cigarette, still hanging off his bottom lip, had burnt down to a stub. "Seeing as you're obviously so tired, I'll take in the supplies."

"The only thing I'm tired of is dealing with your crap," replied Griff, folding his arms and sliding down further in his seat. "But, the job's all yours, rook. After today, you'll be lucky to even get a job delivering sandwiches, so you may as well get in some practice."

CHAPTER 9

Despite being partially buried in the dusty soil of Brahms Three, the alien wreck still stretched out for kilometers. When viewed from the air it already looked immense, but seen up close and personal it was truly awe inspiring. And Hudson couldn't have been any closer than he was at that moment. He was standing on the landing pad outside the RGF guard station on the highest point of the dorsal hull.

The surface of the ship had the smooth, but slightly glassy appearance of igneous rock. It felt like he was standing on the site of an ancient volcanic eruption that would have put Vesuvius to shame. However, unlike the chaotic result of a volcanic eruption, there was order and symmetry to the landscape. It was clearly artificial, and not forged through any natural process. Hudson was in reverence of whatever species had accomplished such a titanic feat of engineering. Yet at the same time he was also baffled at how such a majestic invention could have come to such an inglorious end, on a sterile, barren planet like Brahms Three. Most of humanity had stopped asking questions such as these decades ago. And if he was honest, Hudson rarely gave them a second thought either. However, with the ship now consuming his view in every direction, it was impossible not to be swept up in the mystery.

"Hey, are you the courier run?"

The shout startled Hudson, and he spun around to see an RGF officer standing outside a fissure in the outer hull. This opening served as the entrance into the inner portions of the ship, where the guard station had been established. Other than the landing pad, the only other hint at the guard station's location was a small observation tower placed on the external hull. This was purely for communicating with the RGF base and vessels, since signals couldn't penetrate inside the alien ship.

Similarly, no tool of human design had been able to penetrate the strange rock-like exterior of the hulks. This meant that the only ways in or out were through existing fissures and cracks in the hull. Scientists had speculated that many of the more regular-shaped openings in the hull could have been the result of weapons fire or powerful, blunt-force impacts. However, since there was no weapon, real or theorized, that could do the damage necessary to pierce the alien hulk's armor, these theories had never gained credibility.

"Yes, that's me," Hudson called back, a little embarrassed at being caught daydreaming. "I have a few boxes of supplies. Where do you want them?"

"Bring them through, will ya?" shouted the guard, who hadn't seemed to notice Hudson's blushes. "I'd give you a hand, but all hell's breaking loose inside. These damn scavengers don't miss any opportunity to try to kill each other, but they're damaging the relics in the process. Hell, I'm sure these bastards would rob and murder their own grandmothers if it got them a better score." And with that the guard disappeared back inside the fissure-like doorway, drawing his sidearm as he went.

Rob and murder their own grandmothers? Sounds like someone I know... thought Hudson. He actually contemplated checking the cockpit to make sure Griff wasn't moonlighting inside the wreck as a relic hunter. Instead, he walked around to the cargo hold to collect the first box of supplies. As he approached, he was greeted with a resonant, nasal drone of snoring floating out from the cockpit. Hudson considered dropping the box accidentally-on-purpose to give the bone-idle asshole a rude awakening, but instead he chose to let him snooze. A sleeping Logan Griff was far less obnoxious than an awake one.

Hudson hoisted the box onto his shoulder – it was heavier than it looked – and struggled on towards the crack in the hull. His pulse started to quicken, realizing that this would be the first time he would actually get to set foot inside an alien wreck.

Navigating through the crack while carrying the heavy box was harder than he anticipated. The outer layer of armor was about five meters thick and slippery as hell underfoot. Hudson stumbled several times before reaching the first of the ship's 'ribs'. These were essentially structural frames on which the outer layer of armor was grafted, like flesh on bone. Hudson puffed out his cheeks while he rested for a moment against the frame of the titanic metal beast. He then lowered the box to his hip and continued on, until he reached the alien hulk's last line of defense.

This final layer of armor was something Hudson had read about, but never actually seen. It was a layer of fluid that flowed beneath the outer armor like a lake. When exposed, it seemed to harden, turning into a glassy, rock-like substance an order of magnitude harder than any Earth-based metal. In liquid form, it was one of the more valuable scores a relic hunter could find, assuming they were fortunate enough to discover a method to siphon it off. Even small amounts circulated through a ship's outer hull, like blood flowing through veins, could provide a significant boost to the vessel's armor rating. As such, it was especially prized by the military. Unfortunately, it was also near impossible to get at. In its hardened form, this substance was virtually impenetrable to even the strongest drill bits. Hudson ran his hand along the smooth, obsidian-like surface as he passed through. He shuddered to think what sort of weapon or impact could have cracked open a section of the hardened fluid two meters thick.

Eventually, sweating and more than a little out of breath from his alien crag-hopping, Hudson reached a strange hexagonal hallway. It was strange because there didn't appear to be any particular floor or ceiling; each surface seemed identical to the other. He continued along the corridor until it widened into a vast open space. Hudson reckoned it was easily the size of a football field, and perhaps three storeys tall. Placed at regular intervals in the room were huge hexagonal towers that had no purpose that Hudson could understand, except perhaps to support the ceiling. The RGF guard station had been set up just inside this space, with partitions and desks and all the furniture that would be common to an RGF base in a scavenger town. Except that in the alien setting of the wreck, everything looked out-of-place and completely perverse. Even more baffling was how they managed to carry all of the gear down in the first place, given how much of a struggle it had been for him to carry one box.

Hudson hauled the supplies over to the nearest desk and set the box down on top. The guard who had called him in from outside appeared to be the only one in the entire stadium-sized room.

"There's fine, thanks," said the guard, who seemed anxious. "You can just put the others next to it."

"What are these towers?" asked Hudson, marveling at the scale and precision of the structures.

"Towers?" queried the guard, who appeared to be distracted by a row of monitors on a desk to his side. He looked up, followed the direction of Hudson's gaze, and then stared back at the monitors again. "Oh, cooling conduits, apparently. More than half the ship is one giant engine and reactor. Or that's what the techs say, anyway."

"Everything okay?" asked Hudson, noticing the beads of sweat on the guard's brow. "Where are the others?"

"They're six levels down, trying to stop two rival relic hunter crews from killing each other," said the guard. "Bloody idiots; they know that if they damage any valuable relics, they'll have to pay for them, but some of these crews hold long grudges."

"Do they often fight each other inside?" wondered Hudson, genuinely curious about the day-to-day life of a relic hunter.

"Yeah, well, no..." said the guard, unhelpfully. "I mean, they're always trying to do each other in, but they're usually more subtle about it. Running gun battles just end up with them either dead or being handed a bill for all the items they wrecked along the way."

Hudson remembered that the insides of alien wrecks were considered neutral territory. As such the regular laws of the planet's controlling faction – in this case the CET – didn't apply. There was only one rule, which was, 'all breakages must be paid for', as if the alien ship was a giant china shop. The relic hunter guild had its own code of conduct, of sorts. At a base level this was, 'Please don't rob or murder other guild members.'. However, as Hudson was now seeing first hand, it seemed that at least some of the scavenger crews didn't really take this pledge all that seriously.

"So, what's up with this lot?" asked Hudson, trying to look at what was being shown on the various monitors. "What's made them all so crazy?"

"I don't know, there's talk of someone maybe having found something new," said the guard, starting to look increasingly flustered. "It's driving them all nuts trying to work out who has it, or even if anyone has it at all."

"Something new?" The image of Ericka's curious crystal relic immediately flashed into Hudson's head. "Like a new relic?"

The guard didn't answer, because just then the sound of gunfire echoed into the space. It seemed to have emanated from one of the dozens of hexagonal corridors leading off into the ship. Many of these plummeted deeper into its guts at forty-five-degree angles.

"Shit, it looks like we have another group headed this way," said the guard, grabbing his radio and clicking open the transmitter. "All units, this is base. I need a team back here now!" He released the button but the speaker produced only the harsh crackle of white noise. "Damn it, this ship is like one giant radio shield; I need to get a cleaner line of sight." The guard started running towards the corridor where the gunfire was coming from. Without really thinking why, Hudson followed, forgetting the reason he was actually there in the first place. "Echo and Delta, do you copy?" the guard called into the radio, while trying to aim its antenna into the sloping corridor. Another ripple of gunfire popped along the corridor. "Backup needed at base, do you read, over? Get back here, damn it!"

Hudson peered down the sloping corridor, which descended maybe twenty or thirty meters to a lower level. Two parallel flights of ladders stretched all the way down, but they looked to have been added on, rather than being part of the original ship. Hudson wondered how anything got around inside the hulk, considering the smooth surfaces and apparent lack of sensible ways to navigate the steep corridors.

While the guard continued to shout increasingly harassed requests into the radio, Hudson was distracted by something moving in the corner of his eye. He stepped a few paces to the side to get a better look beyond the nearest cooling tower. He saw three men running out of one of the other hexagonal corridors, heading towards the RGF guard station. The hairs on the back of Hudson's neck prickled. He reached down and unclipped his sidearm, realizing that none of these new arrivals were wearing RGF uniforms.

"Hey, we've got company," Hudson said to the guard, as he drew his weapon.

The guard looked over and cursed, but by this point the trio had also spotted them. "RGF, stop right there!" Hudson shouted, aiming his weapon at the group. He barely recognized his own voice, due to the alien acoustics of the room, and he came off sounding more threatening than he'd intended. He'd merely planned to establish authority, but instead it was like he'd issued a final warning.

One of the relic hunters slid to a stop and held out his arm, causing his companions to fall in behind. There was an awkward silence, and for a moment Hudson thought the relic hunter was going to call back to him. Instead he lifted a compact sub-machine gun from the inside of his long coat and fired.

Hudson hit the deck as rounds pinged off the strange alien metal, making noises like a drunk percussionist. The guard was hit and yelled out in pain as the round sank into his shoulder. Clasping a hand over the wound, the man staggered back, tripping over the lip of the steep corridor. By a stroke of luck, he missed the ladders and instead slid the thirty meters to the lower level, as if he was taking a ride on some sort of alien funfair. However, while the slide down might have looked fun, the heavy thud as the guard smashed into the surface at the bottom wouldn't have been.

Hudson returned fire, causing the three relic hunters to splinter, but now all of them were firing back, and the rounds were landing closer by the second. Hudson crawled over to the edge of the sloping hexagonal corridor and peered down. The guard was moving; neither the bullet nor the drop had killed him. *This guy should buy a lottery ticket tonight...* Hudson thought, hoping his luck would hold out too. However, no amount of luck was going to allow him to win in a firefight against three more heavily-armed relic hunters.

Hudson swallowed hard and made a decision. He hoped this one, unlike so many of his other recent choices, would go in his favor. He pulled himself to the lip of the sloping corridor, flinching as rounds landed all around him, and threw himself over the edge.

CHAPTER 10

Air rushed past Hudson's face as he accelerated out of control down the sloped corridor. He wasn't averse to the thrills and spills of travelling at speeds that would make most people queasy. However, when piloting a spacecraft, he had control – here he was at the mercy of gravity. Panic was building even faster than his velocity as he threw out his hands and feet, desperately trying to slow his descent. Finally, he managed to press the rubber soles of his boots against the smooth surface of the corridor, creating just enough friction to act as a brake. Even so, when he hit the bottom, he hit it hard, rebounding into the far wall like a pool ball bouncing off a cushion.

Despite the momentum of the impact, the majority of the damage was to Hudson's ego. He was embarrassed at how frightened the alien flume had made him feel. However, since it was only his pride that was bruised, he was able to recover quickly. He pulled the guard's body away from the foot of the slope, so that if the relic hunters did peer down, they wouldn't see him, and recovered his weapon. Panic had forced him to let go of it during the slide down to the lower level. Other than appearing concussed the guard didn't seem badly injured. Hudson placed the man into the recovery position and then unclipped the radio from his belt. He cycled through all of the pre-set frequencies, but all he heard was static. Cursing under his breath, Hudson switched the radio to the RGF emergency frequency and placed it beside the unconscious guard. If the man recovered before Hudson managed to escape and send a rescue team, maybe his luck would continue and he'd be able to radio for help.

Next, Hudson assessed his location in detail for the first time since arriving like an out-of-control bowling ball. He observed that the corridor split into four a short way ahead. He wandered over, noting that two other steeply-sloping corridors broke off from each of the four new passages, leading both further into the belly of the giant ship and back up again. Some of the corridors had ladders, others used what looked like vacuum suction clamps stuck to the walls, with ropes attached. Unfortunately, Hudson saw that all of these led to lower levels, rather than back up. It seemed clear that for humans to navigate the alien interior, it required the same sort of skill set that a mountaineer or ancient tomb raider might have possessed.

Rather than venture deeper into the ship, Hudson decided to stay on the same level. He headed along the corridor that ran parallel to the one he'd entered through. Soon, the vast cooling towers were visible again, plummeting through the levels into what Hudson assumed was likely to be the engine section of the ship. This level was shallower than the vast chasm directly above, and the only light came from a collection of dim lamps. These seemed to have been tied around the towers by former relic hunters or perhaps RGF officers. Hudson had never visited the ancient tombs of Egypt or the Aztec tombs in Mexico. He imaged that entering either, alone and in near-darkness, would elicit similar feelings of fear and dread to those he was experiencing now.

The sound of gunfire from one of the myriad new corridors snapped him back to attention. He gripped his weapon more tightly, remembering what the guard had told him. It seemed that some of the relic hunters were still engaged in a pitched battle. And as he'd discovered only a short time earlier, the RGF uniform offered him no protection in this near-lawless place.

Moving swiftly to the far wall, he edged along it with his back pressed flat to the metal. Eventually, he reached another of the many corridors that permeated the ship. Glancing along the corridor he saw what looked like a rope dangling down from an intersecting passage that cut through on a sharp diagonal. If he could get to the rope then maybe he could climb back up to the top level and slip away. Part of him wanted to stay and help the RGF get control of the situation. In part, this was because the inside of the alien wreck was so fascinating and exciting that he didn't want to leave yet. Yet he was acutely aware that Griff may already have woken from his snooze and noticed his absence. More importantly, he was also conscious of being ready to initiate the plan he'd arranged with Ericka. So as much as it saddened him to do so, he had to get out of the remarkable alien ship sooner rather than later.

He crept along the corridor towards the dangling rope with his weapon at low ready. However, as he got closer, he realized that escaping that way was not going to be as simple as he had thought. The corridor had been sheared apart, possibly from the impact of the crash, creating a canyon-like fissure that cut through the bulkhead as far as he could see in either direction. The rope hung tantalizingly just out of reach in the middle of the crevasse.

"Great, which idiot decided this was a good place to hang a rope?" said Hudson, as he stepped to the edge and peered up and down the fissure. Above, he could see light filtering inside from the twin suns of Brahms Three. The crack had evidently split the outer hull too. Looking down, he observed that the fissure seemed to extend at least three or four levels. The gloomy conditions made it difficult for Hudson to judge the depth accurately, like staring into black lake water at midnight. The fissure wasn't especially wide – perhaps two meters at most. Hudson sighed as another crazy idea sprang into his mind. *Why don't I just make a jump for the rope?*

Gunfire again reverberated along the corridor, louder and more frantic than before. Faced with a death-defying leap across an alien chasm, or a running gun battle with who knew how many frenzied relic hunters, he decided the former was the least crazy option. Hudson holstered his weapon and fastened the strap before taking a few paces back. He rubbed his hands together, as if he was some sort of Olympic athlete, preparing for his first (and in this case only) attempt at the high jump.

"Here goes nothing..." said Hudson into the curiously cooler air of the ship's interior. He then sprinted forward and leapt for the rope. His judgment of the height and distance was good, and his hands closed tightly around the cord. Then to his horror his grip slipped, as if the surface was covered in a thin coating of ice or grease. Panic gripped him even tighter than his fingers were squeezing the rope, but it was no use. Hudson slid from the end and plummeted down into the black fissure. By sheer dumb luck, his trajectory slotted him into another angled corridor and he slid along it, yelling and squawking in terror as the animal part of his brain took over. The corridor then spat him out unceremoniously into another cavernous space. He skidded across the floor like an ice hockey puck, eventually coming to rest on his back, eyes wide and gasping for air.

For a few seconds Hudson simply lay there, paralyzed by the huge surge of adrenalin that had flooded into his veins. His mind was completely unable to process what had just happened. Then the precise, orderly clack of bootsteps approaching woke his senses like an ice bucket over the head. He scrambled away from the noise and tried to stand, but then felt a boot press into the small of his back, pushing him down again. He spun over and found himself staring up at a woman, wielding what appeared to be an antique-revolver. She pulled back the hammer and pointed it squarely at Hudson's heart.

CHAPTER 11

Hudson slowly raised his hands in a gesture of surrender and tried to get to his feet, but the woman simply placed her heavy black boot on his chest and pinned him back to the floor.

"Nuh uh uh, I don't think so, clobber," said the woman. She was wagging the barrel of her revolver at him as if it were a finger being wagged at a naughty schoolboy. "Your thieving RGF friends are all the way down in the central core, so what's a lonesome clobber like you doing up here? A bit of illegal freelance prospecting, perhaps?"

She was dressed in what looked like traditional willow-green hunting clothing, but her slim fitting jacket and pants had a soft sheen to them. It resembled goat's leather or a synthetic equivalent. The material looked flexible, but also tough, and the woman wearing it looked the same. From the force with which the boot was pressed down on his chest, Hudson could tell she was strong. In many ways, she reminded him of a younger version of Martina from the Landing Strip.

"If I told you the truth, you wouldn't believe me," said Hudson, his chest now starting to throb under the weight of the woman's leg.

"I could just shoot you now if you prefer?" the woman replied, with a casual nonchalance.

"Not really," said Hudson, "though, do you mind not using me as a doormat while I explain?"

The woman regarded him for a second or two, as if he was an exhibit in a zoo. Then she lifted her leg off his chest and took three measured paces back. "Toss your sidearm away and then get up, but do it *real* slow," she said, keeping the antique weapon trained on him.

Hudson carefully removed his weapon with finger and thumb and flung it to his side, before he climbed to his feet. The dull throb where the heel of the woman's boot had dug into his solar plexus began to subside. The relief was short-lived as the aches and pains of a dozen other knocks and scrapes reasserted themselves.

"You do know that threatening an RGF officer probably isn't the smartest idea you've had today, right?" said Hudson. He then stretched his weary limbs and rubbed aching muscles.

"RGF officers don't patrol these wrecks alone," replied the woman. She was clearly not intimidated by Hudson's threat. Then she looked at him more thoughtfully. "My guess is that you're a hunter trying to pass himself off as a clobber," she added. "So, it's probably best if I shoot you now. I doubt anyone would miss you, especially not me."

"Maybe you could do that," replied Hudson, playing it as cool as he could manage. Considering he was being held at gunpoint while lost inside a city-sized alien space ship, he thought he was doing pretty well. "But if you're wrong, I doubt the other 'clobbers' would look kindly on a scavenger who gunned down a fellow cop. Who knows, such a deed might even come back to bite you. I imagine it'll be tough to get a good score if the RGF are constantly on your ass, looking for some payback..."

The corner of the woman's mouth turned up and her dark eyes narrowed. Both were only fractional adjustments to her otherwise stony expression. However, it was enough to suggest that Hudson's cool, passive-aggressive comeback had amused or intrigued her in some way. Perhaps she simply hadn't expected such steel from Hudson. It was certainly true that he was an atypical example of an RGF cop.

"Maybe you're right," the relic hunter admitted, with a little shrug of her eyebrows. "But this is a big ship; easy for a clobber to get lost in. Perhaps you just fell to your death? No-one would ever find you, or go looking."

"Maybe my friends would miss me?" said Hudson. Outwardly, he'd maintained his poker face, despite his insides wobbling like jelly. He just hoped his tough talking was enough to convince this formidable-looking mercenary not to kill him.

"We both know you don't have any friends," the woman replied, coldly.

Hudson winced, "Ouch..."

"And RGF cops don't care about each other, so nice try, but no dice." She lifted the barrel of the revolver a little higher so that it was now aimed at Hudson's head. Curiously, though, her body had adopted a more casual posture, which made her seem a little less threatening. "So, let's hear it, clobber. You have ten seconds to explain who you really are and why you're here, before I blow you away."

"Fine, just promise not to blow me away if you don't believe what I tell you."

"No promises..." the relic hunter replied.

Hudson rattled through the story of his arrival as quickly as he could. The woman listened intently, her serious midnight-blue eyes not leaving Hudson's for a second. She didn't even blink. By the time Hudson had finished, her lips had adopted a soft, Mona Lisa smile that didn't suit her. Hudson reasoned that she wasn't the sort of person that smiled often, and took this is a positive omen.

"They grease the ropes, sometimes," the woman said, aiming the revolver off to the side and de-cocking it.

"I'm sorry, what?" said Hudson, slightly thrown by her peculiar response.

"Relic hunters," the woman clarified. "We leave traps for other scavenger crews, to catch out the unwary ones, like you."

Hudson laughed, "Come on, you don't expect me to believe that?!" However, the unamused look on the woman's face suggested otherwise. "That has to be illegal? And it's certainly immoral!"

"Immoral, yeah; illegal, no. Anything goes in here, cop," said the woman. "You'd better get used to that."

"And so should you..."

Both of them spun around to see a group of three other hunters emerge from behind a column to their rear. Hudson had been too distracted telling his story to hear them approach. And from the surprised and angry look on the woman's face, it seemed she had been similarly blindsided.

"Tory Bellona... I should have known you'd be involved," said a craggy-looking older man, who strode out in the lead. He wore a military combat vest in a vintage DPM pattern over the top of a tight black tank top. The outfit seemed intentionally designed to highlight the man's arms, which were bigger than most people's thighs. His hands gripped the lapels of the vest, as if he were attempting to accentuate the size of his biceps to look even more intimidating than he already did. His two younger companions, both men who bore a clear family resemblance to the older leader, stood to either side. Both of them aimed nine millimeters at the woman who had been addressed as Tory.

"Holy shit, Rex, you're like a turd that won't flush away," said Tory, whose expression had hardened like granite again. "No matter how many times I try, you always seem to float back to the surface."

"Colorful, as always," replied the older man, smirking. "Now, why don't you give me whatever you and the clobber are working on smuggling out of this place. I'll bet it's the new score, right?"

"Wrong again, shithead," said Tory, "I don't even know this guy. He's just some dumbass that got lost." Hudson saw Tory's muscles tense up and her hand tighten around the grip of her revolver. "And now it's your turn to get lost, Rex. And take your inbred little brethren with you."

"Drop it, Tory," said the older man, lowering his right hand and hovering it over his own holstered weapon. "You might be a good shot, but there's no way you'll get all three of us. Not with that antique piece, not before you're pumped full of holes."

"Maybe I will," said Tory with a composed coolness that Hudson found remarkable, and enviable given the circumstances. "Why don't we find out?"

Red dots appeared on Tory's chest as the younger two relic hunters both enabled laser sights on their weapons. "Be my guest..." said the older man, his smirk twisting into something much more sinister.

Hudson could see that the two younger men were nervous, and that their fingers were resting on the triggers. Nerves and itchy trigger fingers were a bad combination. Tory appeared to recognize the danger as being real too, and backed down. She tossed her antique firearm to the deck while letting out a frustrated growl.

"So, what's the real deal with your pet clobber, here?" said Rex, as one of the red dots swept onto Hudson's chest. "I thought you already had a partner?"

"And I thought you already learned not to cross me, Rex," said Tory. "I see you haven't managed to replace the rest of your crew. You know, the ones I killed the last time we met?"

The two younger hunters glanced at each other uneasily, and Tory smiled at them both. "I left you two pumpkins alive out of pity for your pop," she teased. And then she glowered back at Rex, "for which you owe me, old man." Rex grunted, but didn't attempt to refute Tory's assertion. "I wouldn't get too comfortable around your dear old dad, if I was you," Tory continued, addressing the younger men once more. "We don't call him tombstone for nothing..."

"Cute, Tory," said Rex, whose wicked smile had contorted into something more resembling a grimace. "Just hand over the artefact, and I'll let you and your pet live."

"I haven't found it," replied Tory, angrily. Though it seemed to Hudson that she was angrier with herself than at Rex. "If I had then I wouldn't still be on this shithole planet, would I?"

"Come on, Tory, you're here with a clobber," said Rex, drawing his own weapon and aiming another red dot onto Hudson's chest.

Hudson resisted the urge to speak up in protest or in defense of himself. Mostly, this was because he didn't think he could compete with Tory's ballsy performance. Also, he was afraid that if he did open his mouth, all that would come out was a timid squeak.

"Clearly you've done a deal to have him move it through the checkpoint district for you," Rex continued, oblivious to Hudson's butt-clenched terror. "I'm not a fool, Tory. Give me the relic, or I will kill you and take it."

"See, now you're talking like a true hunter," said Tory, in a mocking tone. "But you should have killed me the moment you saw me, because now, you've given me time to do this."

While Rex had been talking, Tory had slowly inched her weapon hand onto her belt and teased out a small capsule from one of the many pouches. Out of the corner of his eye, Hudson just caught sight of Tory flicking the capsule towards the trio of hunters, like tossing a coin, and he immediately shut his eyes. He knew what was coming; Tory had just dropped a glimmer, the slang name for what was essentially a mini flash grenade. They were illegal on all CET planets. However, Hudson had also worked as a courier on the Outer Portal Worlds, where glimmers were often used in flyer jackings.

It was another incredibly ballsy move from Tory, with no guarantee of success, and every chance of getting them killed if it went wrong. However, Hudson knew one thing for certain; all hell was about to break loose.

CHAPTER 12

The glimmer hit the deck a second later, releasing a powerful concussive blast and a blinding flash of white light. The flash only lasted for a fraction of a second, but despite having closed his eyes, Hudson was still rocked by the intensity of the glimmer's powerful bang. He staggered back, opening his eyes again to see that Tory had also wavered off-balance. Given how close she'd been to the glimmer, Hudson was amazed that she was still standing at all.

A weapon fired, barely audible over the ringing in his ears. Hudson saw that one of the other two hunters was literally shooting blind. Acting on pure instinct he rushed him, grabbing the weapon and then slamming a forearm into his nose. Then Hudson was punched or kicked in the small of his back. He tumbled forward, but recovered just in time to dodge out of the way of another wild shot from the second son. Hudson rushed forward again. Using the pistol he'd taken from the first assailant as a club, he smashed the grip into the side of his attacker's head. As the young man fell, Hudson glanced up and saw Tory and Rex squaring off against each other, trading blows. The younger hunters may have been blinded by the glimmer, but the more experienced older scavenger seemed to have been less affected.

Hudson watched as Tory soaked up a couple of hard hits, but then blocked and countered with a sharp cross that stunned the larger man. Tory pounced on the opportunity, ducking low and sweeping Rex's legs from under him. The brawny man hit the deck hard, and before he knew what had happened, Tory was standing over him. She'd recovered her antique single-action revolver and was pointing it at Rex, eyes burning like liquid fire. She clenched her teeth and clicked back the hammer.

"Woah, woah, you got him!" cried Hudson, hobbling to her side. The other two hunters were still out cold.

"That's not how this works," spat Tory, keeping her eyes fixed on Rex, who lay still, blood trickling from a cut above his left eye. "If I leave him alive, he'll just come after me again some other time."

"And you'll get the better of him again," said Hudson, practically pleading with her. "You shoot him now, like this, and it makes you no better than he is."

"What makes you think I *am* better than him?" snarled Tory, now looking at Hudson, "You don't know me. You don't know what I am."

Hudson removed the cuffs from his belt and crouched down beside Rex. The older man looked confused, but not afraid, and he remained silent.

"What are you doing?" asked Tory. "Get out of the way, or I'll shoot you too."

Hudson flipped over the still-dazed body of Rex, which took more effort than he had anticipated on account of his considerable bulk. Then he cuffed Rex's hands behind his back, and glanced at the female hunter. "When his two sons wake up, they'll set him free. You'll be long gone by then." He stood up and looked into Tory's still fiery eyes. "Come on, Tory, don't do this."

"Since when did RGF cops give a shit about killing hunters?"

Hudson laughed, weakly, "I guess I'm not your average clobber."

The corner of Tory's mouth curled slightly once again, and some of the fire went out of her eyes. She de-cocked her revolver for a second time and holstered it, before folding her arms tightly across her chest. "Okay, but only because you helped me take them down. And I'm still going to rob them for everything they have."

"That's the spirit," said Hudson, realizing the lesser of two evils was as good as he could have hoped for.

"You hear that, Rex?" Tory called over to the handcuffed relic hunter, "This clobber just saved your life."

"Gee, thanks, why don't you give him a damn medal or something?" said Rex, laying on the sarcasm thickly.

Tory then removed a small pistol from a pocket on the rear of her belt. Hudson eyed it suspiciously, but before he could question its purpose, Tory aimed and shot a dart into Rex's huge left arm. The man grunted and then shuffled around so he could look Tory in the eyes.

"You rob me and this isn't... over Tory..." Rex went on, slurring his words more aggressively as the sentence progressed. "Me and you... have... unfinished... business..." Rex then went quiet and lay completely still. A thick line of drool wept from the corner of his mouth.

"A tranq dart?" queried Hudson, and Tory winked at him, before replacing the small pistol in its pouch.

"Less chance of damaging the merchandise than if I blast holes in them with this." She tapped the holstered revolver on her hip.

"I'm not even going to ask how you got that," said Hudson. Though he couldn't help but imagine that Tory probably pried it from the cold, dead hands of another relic hunter. "Now, assuming you're not going to tranq, rob or kill me, I don't suppose you can help me get the hell out of this wreck?".

Tory raised an eyebrow and then pointed to a corridor on the far side of the room. "Take that passage, then second left, next right and you'll find a sloping corridor that leads back to the top level. There's a ladder already in place." Then she smiled, "One that's not booby trapped."

"Good to hear, thanks," said Hudson. "Promise me you're not going to shoot them once I've gone?"

"I don't make promises, remember?" replied Tory, but then before Hudson could complain, she added, "But I'll consider it."

"I guess that will have to do," said Hudson, smiling. Then he recovered his weapon and set off towards the corridor that Tory had indicated, before stopping and turning back. Something Rex had said earlier had just bubbled to the front of his mind. In all the excitement, he'd almost forgotten it. "What was it that Rex thought you had?" Hudson asked, wondering if it was related to Ericka's find. "A relic of some kind?"

"Why do you care?" said Tory, who was already crouched by the side of Rex and going through his pockets. "You interested in turning your coat and becoming a scavenger?" She pulled out a variety of alien artifacts and started placing them into the many pockets of her jacket.

"I'd probably make a better relic hunter than I am an RGF cop," laughed Hudson.

"That's not really saying much, is it?" replied Tory with a healthy dollop of snark. Then she seemed to notice Hudson's hurt expression and took a brief interlude from her thieving activities to answer his question. This was probably more out of pity than guilt for hurting his feelings. "Rumor has it someone found a new relic on this wreck; some kind of crystal shard. Something no-one has seen before." She turned back to Rex and started rifling through his webbing pouches. "Scores like that can make your career."

Hudson was grateful that Tory wasn't looking at him at that moment, because his face went white as chalk. *Ericka's crystal?* He thought, wondering if Tory could possibly be talking about the same item. *If other relic hunters know about it then Ericka could still be in danger...*

"I'll have to remember that," said Hudson, managing to control his voice. He didn't want to tip off Tory that he knew more about the crystal than he'd let on. "Anyway, I'll see you around, Tory Bellona. Thanks for the directions, and for not killing me."

"Hey!" Tory called back, and Hudson stopped again, heart in his mouth. "What's your name, clobber?"

"Hudson," Hudson called back. "My name is Hudson Powell."

"Nice to meet you, Hudson Powell," said Tory, returning to her acts of pillage. "Do me a favor and stay the hell out of my way from now on..."

CHAPTER 13

Much to his relief, Tory's directions had been accurate, as was her assertion that the ladder up to the top level wasn't booby-trapped. Hudson found it ironic that one of the most trustworthy people he'd met since arriving on Brahms Three was a relic hunter. Though he had a feeling that there was more to Tory Bellona than he'd seen. And despite the fact she'd threatened to kill him, he found himself liking her.

Despite almost being shot (twice) and nearly falling to his death (also twice) his first experience inside an alien wreck had been intoxicating. He now understood with absolute clarity why relic hunters would risk their lives again and again to plummet into the depths of these alien machines. It wasn't only the promise of finding a big score, though that itself was alluring, but the thrill of exploring a new frontier. Hudson had been to dozens of portal worlds, and seen more of the galaxy than most people. And while each world had its unique charms, a planet was a planet was a planet, no matter where in the galaxy it was. The alien wrecks, on the other hand, were truly wonderous, and truly the definition of alien.

Even so, he'd had his fill of extra-terrestrial architecture, at least for the time being. Pulling himself up and out of a crack in the outer hull, Hudson was again met with the oppressive, sweaty heat of Brahms Three's twin suns. He got his bearings and saw the RGF patrol craft, still parked on the pad outside the guard station. He was too far away to spot if Griff was still inside, and he couldn't see him prowling around on the outer hull, either. However, wherever he was, Hudson estimated the chances of him being pissed off at pretty much one hundred percent.

Hudson scrambled across the rock-like surface of the alien ship and dropped down in front of the guard station. He could see the patrol craft more clearly now, and Griff wasn't there. Hudson reasoned that the only other place he could have logically been was inside the guard station. So, reluctantly, he made his way back over to the gaping fissure in the hull. *Maybe I'll get lucky and find out that one of the relic hunters took him hostage. Or, even better, shot him full of holes...* Hudson thought to himself, but he knew it was wishful thinking.

Hudson again struggled to traverse the slippery armor plates and solidified liquid armor of the alien ship. Soon, he began to hear the murmur of voices from inside the cavernous space that housed the guard station. And he was able to clearly discern the cantankerous, nasal intonations of his crooked training officer. He took a deep breath and headed inside, ready to face the music. *At least I'll be able to find out if the guard was found alive,* Hudson mused. He was thinking of the RGF officer that met him initially and who had fallen heavily down the sloped corridor.

As he approached the guard station, he could see that at least six RGF officers were now in the room. There were also four relic hunters that had their hands cuffed behind their backs. Three of them were Rex and his two sons, but he couldn't quite make out the fourth. Worrying that it might have been Tory, he changed direction in order to get a better look, but it wasn't her. And to his surprise he discovered that he felt relieved. He could also see the guard who had fallen down the corridor, lying on an improvised cot bed. He had bandages wrapped around his head and was being attended to by a medic, but he was awake and appeared well. Hudson was about to head over and check on him, when he caught sight of Griff. His training officer was red-faced and sweaty, piles of supply boxes stacked at his side. A half-smoked cigarette poked out of his thin mouth, with another six burned-out stubs littering the deck around his feet.

"Where the hell have you been?" Griff shouted over, plucking the cigarette from his lips and throwing his hands out wide. He didn't wait for Hudson to answer, and just jabbed a yellowed finger at his own shoulder. "Do you see these stripes, rook? These are my, 'I don't carry boxes of crap inside alien space ships' stripes. You see what's wrong with this picture?"

"Hey, I'm sorry," said Hudson, though he wasn't sorry at all. The fact that Griff had been required to lug the supplies inside himself amused him greatly, though he knew better than to show it. "It's not like I planned to get shot at by a band of lunatic relic hunters, and then fall thirty meters down a shaft. I've been lost in this ship for well over an hour."

"And yet here you are, alive and well," growled Griff, "The least you could have done was break your damn neck or catch a bullet or two, but you can't even get that right!"

Hudson felt like shoving Griff down one of the angled corridors, but instead he bit his tongue and accepted the verbal beating. He didn't want to anger Griff any further, and cause more delay. The adventure inside the alien wreck had distracted him from the real reason he was out here, which was to help Ericka escape. He felt guilty that he'd almost forgotten about her and their plan. And he felt guiltier still that his thoughts were currently more consumed by images of the fearsome and formidable Tory Bellona. Yet if he dallied for much longer inside the wreck then he risked missing the message from Ericka. If that happened then another RGF patrol craft would be tasked to intercept her. Hudson knew she would then not make it back to the portal, and be captured instead. All of her finds would be seized, and more than likely she'd also end up in a cell, or worse, dead. That would end any hope of helping her brother, and Hudson would be responsible. That was something he didn't want to have to live with.

"Well, I'm here now, so let's just get on with the patrol," said Hudson. "The sooner it's over, the sooner you're rid of me, right?"

Griff scowled at him, "What's the deal with you, rook? Any normal person would bum off on their last day before getting fired. Yet here you are playing hero and 'doing your duty' as if you're bucking for promotion."

"I'm sorry that I fail to meet your desperately low standards," said Hudson, with more snark than he'd intended. And he could see that it had only pissed off Griff more.

"Just get back to the ship and get us airborne," growled Griff. He then grabbed a bottle of water and a fistful of snacks from one of the supply boxes, before storming past Hudson towards the exit. "And don't push your luck any more than you already have. There are worse things than getting fired from the RGF."

There wasn't even an attempt to veil the threat, but Hudson let it slide. He waited for Griff to slip further ahead so that he had space to clear his head and run through the plan in his mind. It was simple enough. He had already given Ericka the RGF patrol routes around the scavenger town and perimeter of the checkpoint district. Ericka would be waiting in her ship, and at the ideal moment, she would blast off and make a run for it. The Shaak radiation detectors around the perimeter would pick up her unregistered claims and the RGF would be alerted to hunt her down.

The Shaak detector was an electronic customs border that surrounded the base and alien wreck site. It worked by measuring the precise quantity of Shaak radiation present on each ship. All ships that arrived in the system were scanned and the exact level of alien radiation was recorded as part of their manifest. The RGF checkpoints would then measure the radiation level of each relic hunter's total score. Any alien items that were transferred to the relic hunters' ships were added to their manifests. Individual hunters arriving on transports were processed in a similar way, except the Shaak levels were recorded on their personal IDs instead. This made it simple to determine whether anyone was attempting to leave the system with undeclared alien tech, no matter how small the amount.

The timing of the operation had to be perfect. Hudson's patrol craft had to be closest to the base when Ericka departed, while the second on-duty patrol craft was on the opposite side of the perimeter. Once Hudson was in pursuit, he'd put on a show of chasing Ericka down, only to be forced to fall back at the last moment with mysterious engine difficulties. By this point, Ericka would be too far ahead for any other RGF ship to catch her. And once she was through the portal, she'd be in the clear.

Hudson may have been a rookie RGF officer, but he'd also paid attention during his lectures at the academy. He knew that for the RGF to prove that Ericka had smuggled undeclared alien artifacts from Brahms Three, they needed to catch her before she left the system. Once she was through a portal, there were dozens of other ways that a hunter could acquire alien tech, thus altering the total level of Shaak radiation on their ship. As soon as the ship passed through another Shaak radiation perimeter, the ship's manifest would be updated. This new level of radiation would then become the baseline.

This system had proved effective at discouraging relic smuggling, but it hadn't stopped it completely. During their eventful night together, Ericka had told Hudson of numerous creative ways in which hunters had managed to smuggle relics past the RGF checkpoints. Ericka's own method had been to hide smaller objects inside the shielded compartment in her jacket. Over several hunts on the wreck at Brahms Three, Ericka had managed to amass an elicit score that was enough to pay off her brother's debts. And this wasn't even including the mysterious crystal that everyone seemed so interested in. The problem was how to get past the Shaak sensor perimeter, and this was where most relic hunters came unstuck. RGF cops may not have been honorable on the whole, but they were trained to be excellent combat pilots. Even a veteran relic hunter would struggle to defeat an RGF patrol craft if it came down to a gun battle. However, with Hudson in control of the pursuit, Ericka's escape was assured.

He climbed up the rear cargo ramp of the patrol craft and entered the cockpit. Griff was already in his customary 'feet up' position, munching messily on one of the snacks he had taken from the guard station. He didn't acknowledge Hudson's arrival, and Hudson decided that keeping his mouth shut this time was a better plan than being a smart ass. Slotting himself down into the pilot's seat, he closed the rear ramp, and powered up the vertical lift engines. The craft ascended into the air above the mammoth alien vessel, and Hudson slotted into their patrol pattern around the wreck site.

His course just skirted past the outer edge of the scavenger town. He peered down at the dingy, narrow streets of Brahms Three's seedy nightclub district and wondered if he'd ever make it out to this distant portal world again. There was no doubt that Brahms Three was a dump, full of the worst sort of cutthroats and villains, with one or two notable exceptions. However, despite cursing Chief Inspector Wash for assigning him to this duty, the last twenty-four hours had been the most thrilling of his thirty-eight years.

"You know, I think I'm going to miss this place," said Hudson. He was thinking of Ma and her dive bar with its impossibly strong whiskey and mix of oddball clientele.

"Tell someone who gives a shit, rook," Griff replied with his mouth full, while tuning one of his console screens to an entertainment feed.

Hudson only half heard Griff's irritable reply. He was now reminiscing about the night he'd spent in the scavenger town the day before. He recalled the adrenalin-soaked rush he'd got from the brawl in the alley, followed by the excitement of learning about the mysterious alien crystal. And then the unexpected, unadulterated thrill of what came after, back in Ericka's hostel room. He had expected this day to be relatively tame in comparison, but how wrong he'd been. In the last couple of hours alone he'd been shot at, got lost in an alien wreck, fallen foul of a booby trap, met another dangerously alluring relic hunter, and gotten into another fight. *Maybe Ma was right*, he wondered. *Maybe I've been doing this all wrong. I shouldn't be policing the relic hunters – I should* be *a relic hunter...*

"Hey, eyes on the road, rook," snapped Griff, who had apparently noticed that Hudson was away in a world of his own. "I don't want you getting me killed, before I see you run out of this outfit like the waste of space you are."

Griff's insults no longer stung. He could call him all the names under this little planet's twin suns and it wouldn't dampen his spirits. Hudson turned away from Griff and peered down at the massive shape of the alien wreck impaled into the dusty-brown soil ahead of them. Its heavily-armored external hull shimmered in the morning sun, like a half-buried, wingless dragon.

"Slotting into patrol plan now," said Hudson, as he swung around and began following the course highlighted in his heads-up display. He checked the location of the second patrol craft, and it was right where it was supposed to be, on the far edge of the checkpoint district.

"Keep it down, will you? I'm trying to watch this," snapped Griff, tearing open a packet of potato chips. He noisily munched on them as he watched the entertainment feed.

Yes sir... Hudson thought, glancing over at Griff. He marveled at how it was possible for one person to be so vile and repugnant. Then out of the corner of his eye he noticed his comms system was flashing. He reached over and pulled the screen closer, before checking the message. It had been sent privately to his secure ID.

'Standing by... Just say the word. Catch you on Earth, sometime? Love, Ericka.'

Hudson smiled and then glanced across to Griff to make sure he hadn't noticed anything. His TO's long legs were still raised up on his console and his bony fingers were still buried deep inside the packet of chips. Griff snort-laughed at whatever humorous show he was watching, and dusty crumbs tumbled from the corners of his mouth onto his shirt and cargo pants.

What a slob... Hudson thought, before turning back to his monitor to tap out a message in reply. "The word is said... Punch it! I'll see you on Earth, and I'm buying." Hudson re-read the message and hovered his finger over the 'Send' button. Once he transmitted the message there would be no turning back, for either of them. However, for the first time in his life there was no-doubt in his mind about what he should do next. He pressed the button, closing the circuit and closing this chapter of his life for good.

CHAPTER 14

Three high-pitched squawks rang out inside the cabin and repeated, rousing Griff from his post-snack nap. He dragged his spindly legs off the console and jolted upright, showering the deck with potato chip crumbs. A burned-out cigarette slid from his thin, chapped lips and tumbled down next to the crumbs. He hastily brushed it off, along with the cigarette ash that had come to rest on his collar, scorching it black. "What the hell? What's going on?!" Griff blurted out, still disorientated from being woken so suddenly.

Hudson leant forward and shut off the alarm, which was repeating on a loop. His heart had already begun thumping long before the alarm had sounded, but now it felt like his chest was about to split open. The alarm signaled that his plan was in motion. It was terrifying, but also thrilling. These were two sides of the same coin, and two sensations he'd gotten to liking over the last couple of days.

Griff rubbed his eyes and checked his console, still unaware of the reason for the alert. Meanwhile, Hudson watched as a thick plume of smoke began to dissipate over the scavenger town. It was the trail of a ship that had hard burned out of the space port only moments earlier. Shortly after, it had pushed through the checkpoint perimeter and triggered the Shaak radiation alarms. It was Ericka's ship, which meant the chase would soon be on.

Go on, Ericka... run hard... run! Hudson urged, glad that Griff's befuddled state had given her a few extra seconds head start. However, it didn't take Griff long to blow the fog from his mind.

"Shit, looks like we've got a smuggler making a run for the portal," said Griff, brushing more crumbs off his uniform and from the corners of his mustache. Then he saw the scorch damage to his collar from the cigarette ash and cursed again. Hudson waited patiently for Griff to rudely bark an order at him, and he soon obliged. "Well, don't just sit there, rook, we're the assigned pursuit craft. Get after it!"

"Yes sir, just waiting for you to wake up a little first, sir," said Hudson, cheerfully. He then pulled back on the control column and forced the throttle pedal to the deck.

"Don't get wise with me, smart ass," Griff hit back, "I don't care if this is your last shift; so long as you wear that uniform, you do as I say, got it?"

"Oh, I've got it. One hundred per cent crystal clear, sir," said Hudson, with an artificial politeness that made him sound borderline insubordinate. He checked the navigation scanner. All of the other RGF ships in the vicinity of Brahms Three were significantly further away, just as planned. "Setting a pursuit course now. No-one else is in range, so it looks like it's down to us."

"No shit, Einstein," Griff snapped, tightening his harness, which he'd loosened earlier to make his snooze more comfortable. Hudson could already tell that he'd rubbed his TO up the wrong way with his cheerfully flippant tone. "If that ship gets away then you can bet your ass my report will cite 'inept piloting' as the reason why," Griff added.

"What do I care if it gets away?" replied Hudson, enjoying pushing Griff's buttons, "I'm quitting anyway, so what difference does it make to me?"

Griff had now gone from distinctly unamused to red-faced and furious. "I've had enough of your crap, rook!" he yelled, jabbing a bony finger at Hudson. "If that ship gets away, you'll end up in a cell. And I'll personally make sure Wash lets you rot on this pigsty of a planet for the next decade."

"Jeez, relax, Griff, I'm joking!" said Hudson, utterly unfazed by the outburst. "Unlike some members of the RGF, I do things by the book, remember? I'll catch the ship; just be ready to do your part."

This seemed to appease Griff, at least a little. "You don't have to worry about me, rook," he said, easing back into his seat. "Just get us in range and I'll do the rest." However, although Griff had backed down, every muscle in his wiry frame was still tensed and brimming with nervous energy.

Soon, the dusty brown surface of Brahms Three shrank into the distance and the view outside the cockpit grew darker. Seconds later the patrol craft passed through the planet's upper atmosphere and into the barren emptiness of space. Hudson had already almost caught up with Ericka's dilapidated light freighter. She was still at least ten minutes away from reaching the portal, and Hudson would be within weapons range in a quarter of that time. He rehearsed the plan in his mind, running through the steps over and over again, including what he intended to say to Griff. *It'll work, Hudson, just relax...* he told himself. *It's going to work...*

Hudson checked his instruments and called over to Griff, "Weapons range in two minutes." He didn't need to provide an update, but Griff had been unusually quiet since they'd reached space. "Shouldn't you radio the runner and order it to stand down?"

Griff was busy fine-tuning the settings on his weapons console. "Are you the one giving me orders now, rook?" he said, without looking up.

"No, it's just procedure," replied Hudson, trying to keep his cool. "You know, by the book?"

"Radio the damn ship if you want," said Griff, impatiently pulling the controls for the forward cannon into position. "But you're wasting your breath." Then Griff glanced over at Hudson while tapping the grip of his manual firing stick. "This is the only language those scumbags understand."

"Fine, I'll do it then," replied Hudson, making a deliberate attempt to sound annoyed at Griff's lack of co-operation. Though it was actually a relief to be the one making the call. He hoped that Ericka hearing his voice on the radio would reassure her that everything was going to plan. He slipped his headset on and flipped open a channel to the light freighter. "Relic hunter vessel, Gulliver – ID November One Five One Four Kilo – this is RGF Patrol Craft Scimitar," Hudson began, watching the range indicator carefully as he spoke. "You are ordered to return to the checkpoint district on Brahms Three immediately. Fail to comply and we will fire on you..." He waited for a response, knowing that one would not come, and sure enough the speaker returned only static.

"Told you so..." said Griff, with a smug look on his craggy face. Hudson couldn't get distracted by thoughts of murdering Griff; time was running out and he needed to act soon. He let go of the control yoke with his right hand and flexed his fingers, pumping the blood to get the circulation flowing.

He was ready to initiate the next stage of the plan. Into the microphone he said, "I say again, relic hunter vessel, stand down and return to the planet or we will fire upon you." However, his inner voice was urging Ericka to hold her course and her nerve. *Keep going Ericka...* he called out in his mind, *you're almost there, just keep running...*

"Thirty seconds to weapons range," Hudson called out, but Griff didn't answer. All of his partner's attention was now focused through the holographic gunsight that had lit up in front of his eyes. With Griff's attention diverted elsewhere, Hudson made his move. Slowly, and with half an eye still on Griff, he reached down underneath his dashboard and felt for the main bus cable. The tips of his fingers made contact with the reinforced casing of the thick metal plug and he teased it back just enough to break the connection. Immediately, the indicators on his dashboard started to flash urgently, his control column went dead and the main engines cut out.

"What the hell are you doing?" Griff called out.

Hudson whipped his hand out from under the dashboard as swiftly as he could, but it was clear that Griff had caught him in the act. "What does it look like?" Hudson hit back, trying to improvise on the spot, and hoping he sounded calmer than he felt. "We just lost flight control, so I'm checking my console. What the hell are you yelling at me for?"

Griff swiveled his chair to face Hudson, and popped open the strap securing his sidearm inside his holster. "Bullshit, rook, I saw your hand under there before we lost power," Griff spat, now resting his palm on the grip of his weapon. "What's going on? What are you trying to pull?"

"My hand was under the console because I was trying to fix it, you moron," protested Hudson. He was fighting hard to suppress the rising wave of panic that had flooded into his body. "It could just be a faulty bus cable or something like that. You know how the RGF skimps on maintenance, especially on these backwater worlds."

Just then the engines kicked back into life as the loosened bus cable wiggled around inside its housing, making intermittent contact with the connectors. The brief burst of acceleration jostled Griff in his seat like a mule bucking its rider. For a split-second, Hudson considered rushing him, before realizing his harness was still fastened. He reached down and pressed the release so that he was ready to move should another opportunity arise. However, when he looked up again, he saw that Griff had drawn his weapon and leveled it at him.

"Keep your ass in that seat, rook," Griff ordered, teasing the end of the barrel towards him. "You're a damn liar. You're going to tell me what you're up to, or you're going to get this bullet."

"Shooting your pilot is hardly a smart plan," said Hudson. He was hoping to call Griff's bluff, or at least stall him some more.

"I can fly this piece of crap well enough, asshole," replied Griff. "Besides, the RGF can always just ferry up a new pilot. So, it honestly doesn't matter to me if you arrive back at Brahms Three in that seat or in a body bag."

Hudson's brain froze up. He'd run out of ideas, but even if he had any more bluffs up his sleeve, he was sure Griff wouldn't believe them. He glanced out of the cockpit glass, watching the blue glow of Ericka's engines grow smaller, urging the ship to go faster.

Griff scowled and followed Hudson's gaze out through the cockpit glass, "You're with the smuggler, aren't you?" he said, suddenly piecing it all together. "You set this up back on the planet. I knew you were up to something!"

"You're delusional..." Hudson began, but Griff was having no more of his objections.

"Save it, rook," he snapped, cutting Hudson off mid-sentence. He then swapped the weapon into his left hand and entered a short sequence of commands into his console. A second later the door to the rear cargo compartment slid open and thumped into its housing.

"Drop your weapon on the deck and then get aft," ordered Griff, gesturing through the open doorway with his sidearm. "I'll deal with you later, once I've taken care of this friend of yours."

Hudson hesitated, considering if there was still a chance to rush Griff while the weapon was in his off hand. However, his partner quickly switched hands again and his opening vanished. He cursed his indecision, because now he was all out of options.

"Make a move, please..." said Griff, aiming the weapon at Hudson again. "I'd love you to give me an excuse to shoot you right here..."

Hudson gritted his teeth and then slid his weapon out of its holster, before dropping it on the deck, all the while being watched closely by Griff.

"Kick it over here," Griff ordered, and Hudson did so, at the same time glancing out of the cockpit glass again. He could just about make out the faint glow of Ericka's engines, but he knew she was still five or six minutes away from the portal. If Griff restored control, he'd still have time to catch her. And if that happened, Hudson knew what would come next, because he'd already witnessed how his sadistic partner dealt with rogue relic hunters.

Suddenly, the patrol craft's engines kicked in again, momentarily kangarooing the ship like a car on the verge of stalling. Griff was forced to lower his weapon and grasp onto the seat frame to keep his balance. Hudson saw his chance and this time he didn't waver. Propelling himself out of his seat like a jack-in-the-box, he dove at Griff as if he was making a football tackle. He had hoped to knock him out or at least badly wind him. Unfortunately, luck was not with Hudson this time. The engines kicked in again, pushing Griff away from Hudson's desperate, outstretched hands. A second later, he slammed into the bulkhead and then hit the deck like a stone.

CHAPTER 15

The cabin dissolved into blackness and for a time – he had no idea how long – Hudson was only vaguely aware of where he was. Slowly his ears started ringing, louder and clearer, and his vision became a blurry white fuzz. He tried to move, but all of his actions felt muddled. He wasn't even sure if he was standing, sitting or flat on his back. He tried to speak, to call out for help, but no words came out.

Deep down, he knew he was in danger, but he couldn't remember why. Then an image of Ericka shot into his thoughts. She was naked, lying on her stomach on top of the bed in her hostel room. There was a half-empty whiskey bottle by her side, and she was smiling at him. *Ericka?* Hudson called out in his mind, but she simply smiled back at him, feet raised up behind her, toes waggling. *What?... Why?...* And then the realization hit him like a jolt from an electroshock ring. *Griff!* The word echoed around his mind, and then the image of Ericka dissolved. It was replaced by the face of Logan Griff, leering down at him, larger than life. *No! Run, Ericka... You have to run... You have to run!*

Hudson waned in and out of consciousness, babbling incoherently, until the deck shuddered, literally shaking some sense back into his bruised head. He could feel himself sliding, until something solid stopped him. His head was now spinning out of control; time seemed to slow down and speed up. It was a nightmare, and he couldn't wake up.

Eventually, his vision started to resolve and he got a sense of his bearings. He was still on the deck in the cockpit of the RGF patrol craft, in a contorted heap. His body was pressed against the bulkhead that separated the cockpit from the rear cargo compartment. He heard a distant, percussive rattle and then the dull, heavy thud of something much closer. Struggling to right himself, he eventually managed to sit up. Through squinting eyes, he saw the face of Logan Griff, surrounded by flashing white patterns, like a halo of stars.

"I should kill you, rook, but I really don't need the heat it would bring down on me," Griff said. He then adjusted his grip on his sidearm so that he was holding it by the barrel instead. "Even I'd struggle to explain away how you ended up getting shot with an RGF gun when there are only two of us on-board. If this was an Outer Portal World, I might get away with it, but the CET are lame-ass 'by the book' guys, just like you, rook. Or should I say 'crook'?" Griff laughed at his own joke, exposing two rows of yellow, warped teeth. "Luckily, I can shoot your relic hunter friend over on that piece of shit freighter without any such trouble," Griff added, his grimy smile beaming wider. Then he bent down, bringing his thin face and wiry mustache so close that Hudson could smell the tobacco on his breath and the sweat soaked into his shirt. Both were unusually intense and unbearably repugnant. He tried to push away from him, but there was no strength in his arms.

"I warned you not to cross me, rook," continued Griff, and the words oozed out like poison from a cobra's fangs. "Like I told you; I always get my cut." Then Griff slashed the sidearm down sharply across the side of Hudson's temple, and the starry halo was replaced by complete darkness.

CHAPTER 16

Hudson opened his eyes and then grimaced as a crippling pain flooded his body, forcing him to shut them again. It was as if a giant needle had been inserted through his temples. It was a full minute before he was able to again force open an eyelid, but the throbbing in his head remained. It was like the hangover from hell; worse even than the morning after a session on Ma's whiskey.

He was cognizant enough to realize he was still in the cockpit of the patrol craft, still slumped up against the bulkhead. He tried to sit up, but his hands and feet wouldn't move. Hudson looked down, and saw they were bound with the same thick, dark grey tape the RGF used to seal up boxes of seized relic claims. He knew the material was too tough to break with brute strength alone. Instead, he began searching around the cockpit for anything he might be able to use to rip or cut through it. It was only then that he realized Griff was no longer with him, and in his absence an eerie stillness filled the air. Even the familiar thrum of the deck plating, vibrating in mechanical harmony with the ship's main reactor, was absent. With the pain clouding his ability to think clearly, it took Hudson a few seconds to realize why – the patrol craft was no longer moving.

A gut-wrenching swell of dread added to the cocktail of physical sensations that Hudson was struggling to process. There could have been any number of reasons why Griff had stopped the ship, but he feared the worst. Then he caught a glimpse of a second ship just visible through the cockpit glass. Panic gripped him, blanking out every other sensation, even the pain. *Please no... please no...* he repeated in his head as he heaved himself into the center of the deck to get a better view. As the shape of the vessel became more distinct, he was consumed with a feeling of grim hopelessness. His body fell limp and his weary head clattered against the cold metal beneath him. There was no doubt it was Ericka's ship. Griff had caught her and there was every chance she was dead already.

Get up... Get up! Hudson urged himself, refusing to permit the darkness to consume him. *There's still a chance... Get up!* He hauled himself upright again and then cried out, "Griff!" It was a near animalistic roar, filled with all the anger and pain and despair that had polluted his every thought.

"Griff, where are you?!" There was no answer. Either Griff was ignoring him, or he was already on-board Ericka's ship. He'd obviously managed to knock out its engines and latch on to the light freighter's docking ring. However, other than this he had no idea what had occurred during the time he had been unconscious. Griff had threatened to kill her; and Hudson knew it wasn't an idle threat.

His roars combined with the awareness of the mortal danger Ericka was in caused adrenalin to surge through his veins. Hudson cried out again, struggling even harder against the restraints, but it was futile and the bonds held fast.

Sucking in heavy gulps of oxygen to fuel his tiring muscles, Hudson closed his eyes and tried to think more clearly. He knew he had to get free before Griff got back to the ship. He'd already witnessed him destroy a vessel just so that he could claim salvage rights. He wouldn't put it past him to do this again. Griff could take all of the valuable claims, uncouple the ships and then blow Ericka's vessel to pieces, with her still inside. *I wouldn't even put it past the crooked bastard to throw me onto her ship too*, thought Hudson. *No witnesses to refute his story...*

He opened his eyes and continued his search for anything in the cockpit that could break his binds. Then he noticed that the seat runners for Griff's chair were exposed. He always kept his seat pushed far forward, despite his lanky frame, so that he could more easily rest his legs up on the center console. Hudson shuffled over to the rear of Griff's seat and managed to lift his bound hands onto the closest of the two sharp rails. He then jostled back and forth in an attempt to saw through the thick tape. *Come on, come on!* he urged as his efforts became more frantic, until eventually he heard part of the tape rip. Encouraged, Hudson pressed harder, bruising and scraping his wrists and hands against the metal until the tape finally gave way completely. Tearing the remains away, he then reached down and unwrapped his ankles, before pushing himself upright. A wave of nausea and dizziness swept over him and he almost collapsed on the spot. Hudson instinctively grabbed the back of Griff's chair, using it like a life buoy to steady himself until the dizziness subsided.

Suddenly, muffled shouts and the sound of metal clanking filtered through the open cockpit door. Without consideration for his own safety, he ran aft and saw that the port-side umbilical was extended. Still unsteady and wavering from one side of the compartment to the other, Hudson pushed on. He almost fell, but managed to catch hold of the docking hatch to again steady himself. He realized a confrontation with Griff awaited him on the other side of the umbilical and reached down for his weapon. Then he remembered that Griff had already forced him to relinquish it. Hudson knew he was in no condition for a fight, but he needed a way to foil his partner's plans. Otherwise, Griff was sure to destroy the relic hunter ship and kill Ericka, and probably him too.

Hudson peered around the rear compartment for inspiration. Spotting the aft emergency communications panel, he had an idea. Staggering over to it, he smashed the thin covering of glass with his fist to activate the distress beacon. Then he hurriedly dialed in the emergency spacecraft frequency for the CET, before opening the channel.

"Mayday, Mayday, Mayday, this is Officer Hudson Powell on the RGF Patrol Craft Scimitar, Scimitar, Scimitar," Hudson began, hoping that he wasn't slurring his words too obviously. His head still pounded like a timpani drum and the constant thumping almost deafened him to his own words. "We have experienced complete engine failure. Immediate assistance required. We have one relic hunter smuggler in custody with undocumented claims. Repeat, one relic hunter smuggler in custody with undocumented claims. Over."

That should get their attention... thought Hudson. If there was one universal truth common to all the controlling authorities, across all the portal worlds, it was money. CET wouldn't give a shit about a stranded RGF vessel. However, if there were claims to be had, Hudson had no doubt that a CET ship would be hard-burning towards them within seconds. He couldn't just sit on his hands and wait for it to arrive, even if that was the smart option, given his concussed condition. He had to know if Ericka was alright, and he had to confront and stop Griff.

Hudson pushed away from the comms panel and made his way through the umbilical connecting the two vessels. Ericka's ship was a small cutter-class light freighter a little over twice the size of the stripped down RGF patrol craft. It was large enough to have living quarters in addition to a small cargo compartment. He knew this style of vessel well from his days as a courier runner, and so knew the quickest route to the hold. Staggering onwards, the sound of shuffling boots and the scrape of objects or boxes being pulled across the deck grew louder. He quickened his pace and practically fell through the open shutter door into the cargo hold. The first thing he saw was Ericka's body, lying just inside the arch. She wasn't moving and blood was visible, smeared across her leather jacket.

"No!" Hudson cried out, throwing himself further into the room and dropping down by her side. He pulled Ericka's limp body next to his and smoothed the hair from her eyes. They remained closed, even as Hudson shook her gently, urging her to wake up.

"You just don't know when to stay down, do you rook?"

Hudson looked up and saw Griff at the far end of the hold. He was rifling through the storage racks as if it was just a normal day on the job.

"What have you done?!" Hudson shouted as Griff carefully placed two more alien relics into an RGF-issue backpack, which was already stuffed full. "You killed her!"

"Quit your crying, she's not dead," Griff yelled back without thinking; but then he seemed less certain of himself. "Well, she wasn't a few minutes ago, anyway." He glanced over to Hudson, still holding Ericka close, and shrugged. "Not that I give a shit if she lives or dies. She's a criminal and got what was coming to her."

Hudson had tried to be smart and tried to stay calm, but he couldn't stomach this hateful man any longer. He was going to tear Logan Griff down, or die trying. Death was no less than he deserved for failing Ericka. He'd agreed to help her. It was his plan. It was his fault.

Hudson began to gently lower Ericka's body to the deck in readiness to charge at Griff, when her hand closed around his wrist. As he looked down, he found her eyes meeting his and was almost overcome with relief.

"I'm sorry, I'm sorry, you'll be okay..." Hudson blabbed, as Ericka's mouth opened. There was a trickle of blood visible at the corner. "Just hang in there, help is coming. You're going to be fine..."

"Help..." said Ericka, her voice barely more than a whisper.

"Yes, that's right," said Hudson, "The CET is on the way. You'll be okay..." Ericka shook her head, and then gently pulled back the lapel of her jacket to reveal the bullet wound in her chest. Hudson pressed his hand over the wound, desperately trying to stop the blood from leaking out of her body. However, he'd seen enough gunshot injuries in his lifetime to know at once that this one was fatal.

"Help him," croaked Ericka. "My brother... please... help him. Hudson... Please..."

"I will, I will," Hudson answered, his words almost frantic. "Just take it easy, okay, you need to save your strength."

The thud of heavy boots on the deck caused Hudson to reluctantly tear his eyes away from Ericka. Griff was now pacing back towards him, body hunched over from the weight of the rucksack on his back. His sidearm was clutched in his sweaty palm, nicotine-stained finger curled around the trigger.

"You did all this for a woman?" asked Griff, peering down at Hudson like he was a lab experiment gone wrong. "You really are the dumbest rook I've ever come across."

Hudson wanted to strangle Griff. He wanted to watch him splutter and beg as he choked the air out of his scrawny neck. Yet he also knew that getting himself killed now wouldn't help Ericka. "You've got your score, Griff. That's all you care about, right?" Hudson countered. It took all he had left not to dive for his throat. "You gain nothing if she dies. It's just more paperwork, right?"

Griff sighed and nodded, "I do hate paperwork," he admitted, but then his eyes narrowed. "But I hate traitorous scumbags like you even more. And that's why I'm going to blow up this ship with both of you on-board."

"I thought you'd be smarter than that," replied Hudson. He was trying to appeal to Griff's well-developed sense of self-preservation. "Just leave me here and I'll be gone out of your life for good. That way no-one comes asking you awkward questions, or goes snooping around and finding stuff you're not supposed to have..."

Griff laughed. "Nice try, rook. Problem is, if I leave this ship intact, my salvage rights go out of the window. Besides, I'm going to enjoy watching you burn in space."

"You won't get away with it, you piece of shit!" spat Hudson. Though he was painfully aware of how unconvincing he sounded.

Griff laughed again, though this was darker and even more sinister. "You know I will. A tragic accident, caused by the umbilical detaching before you got back on board. Then a reactor overload caused by the engine damage after I disabled the ship and... boom!" He laughed again, and then itched his moustache with the barrel of his weapon, as if it were an extension of his bony finger. "Wash will sign off on whatever I say, especially after I give her a fat slice of what's in this bag." Griff smiled as he let it all sink in, and then added, "Money talks, rook. I tried to tell you, but you were too dumb to listen."

Hudson knew he had to stall Griff for as long as possible. His only chance now was for the CET to arrive before Griff made good on his threats. He was about to argue back when he felt Ericka's hand slip from his arm. He looked down and her eyes stared back up at him, except now they were blank and glassy.

"Ericka?" Hudson said, softly at first, and then louder and more forcibly. "Ericka, please answer me..." he tried again, shaking her gently and causing her head to loll to the side. He placed a finger against her neck to feel for a pulse, but the only movement he detected was the trembling of his own body.

"See what crossing me gets you?" said Griff, with an icy indifference to what he'd just witnessed. "Her death is on you, rook."

Hudson barely heard Griff's voice; he was still gripped by the sight of Ericka's now lifeless body. He'd promised to help her, and to help her brother, but he'd only succeeded in getting her killed. He turned to Griff, staring into the barrel of the weapon that was now pointed at his head, finger

146

adding pressure to the trigger. Hudson wasn't afraid; perhaps, he even deserved a bullet. However, he'd be damned if Logan Griff would be his executioner. If he was going to die, alongside Ericka, he'd make Griff fight for it. He'd make him feel it.

Suddenly the cargo hold of the light freighter was filled with an authoritarian-sounding voice. The sound was filtering in through the open umbilical to the RGF patrol craft.

"RGF Patrol Craft Scimitar, this is Commander Roach of the CET Corvette Galatea. We are responding to your distress beacon." The voice was calm and professional. "We have you in our sights now; remain in position and await our arrival."

Griff scowled and inched his weapon lower so that he could meet Hudson's eyes more clearly. "You alerted the CET?"

"Sorry to spoil your plans, asshole," replied Hudson. He took a sliver of comfort from knowing that at least he'd denied Griff from claiming Ericka's score. The CET would seize and impound the entire contents of the hold and then auction it off at a later date. RGF would only get a twenty percent cut, of which Griff's money-grabbing hands would see precisely zero. "I'm afraid your salvage rights just went out the airlock."

"Yeah, well so will you soon," Griff spat back, "Once I've put a bullet through your thick skull."

Hudson laid Ericka's body gently onto the deck and pushed himself to his feet. He felt groggy and nauseous, like someone had spun him around and around on an office chair for the last ten seconds. Griff took two paces back, aiming the weapon at Hudson's body, finger still on the trigger, but his eyes betrayed his doubt.

"You can't kill me now, and you know it," said Hudson, struggling to focus on Griff's lined face. "I'm sure you can come up with a convincing lie about why you had to shoot a relic hunter smuggler. But you can't explain away shooting your own partner, no matter how you spin it."

Griff's top lip twitched, animating his wiry mustache as if he was about to sneeze. "What if I tell them about your little deal with the smuggler lady here?" he added, eyes flicking down to the body at Hudson's feet.

Hudson refused to look down; the pain and guilt and shame was still too raw. He feared that seeing Ericka's lifeless eyes again would pitch him into the dark precipice he'd been teetering on the edge of since discovering Griff's crime. Hudson still wasn't afraid of him, or his petty threats. Griff could do nothing more to him now, not without further worsening his own prospects.

"No, you won't," Hudson answered, ejecting each word like a bullet. "You will keep your mouth shut, or I'll have a lot to say to Commander Roach about all the claims you've stolen from the CET. It wouldn't take much of an investigation to expose you for the thief you are. So, take me down, and I take you down with me. And we both know who'd fall the hardest and deepest."

Griff's finger was still wrapped around the trigger. The pressure of a gentle breeze was all that was needed to activate it, but Griff just managed to hold back. "The RGF will still get its cut of your girlfriend's crappy score," Griff answered. He then lowered his weapon by a fraction and slid his trigger finger back onto the frame. "But you've cost me today, and I won't forget that. It doesn't matter where you go, I'll find you and one day you'll pay. I promise you that."

"I don't owe you a damn thing," Hudson growled, turning his back on Griff and heading out of the cargo bay. He reached the corridor leading back to where the patrol craft was docked, but hesitated, compelled to take one last look at Ericka. His hand tightened around the door frame, squeezing the blood from his fingers so that his knuckles went white. He peered up at Griff, seeing a face that would now forever be etched into his memory, his waking thoughts and his dreams too. The face of a murderer. The face of someone who, no matter how long it took him, would pay for what he'd done. "And you won't need to come looking for me, because I'll find you," Hudson added, darkly. "We have unfinished business..."

CHAPTER 17

The last few hours had been the hardest of Hudson's thirty-eight years. Although his plan to alert the CET had saved his life, he now had to follow through with the lie that they needed help. Far worse was having to tow the line with Griff's more sinister falsehood about how Ericka had died. Hudson sorely wanted to expose Griff as the cowardly murderer he was, but doing so would only reveal his own conspiracy to defraud the CET and the RGF. It wouldn't be difficult for a CET court to find evidence that Hudson and Ericka had known each other. Besides, there were communication logs between the two ships that would also indicate his guilt. So, he had no choice but to let Griff walk away this time. However, Hudson would never forget, or forgive, his crime.

Hudson and Griff stayed well clear of each other while the CET engineers checked the RGF Patrol

Craft. They found the loose bus cable within minutes, and enjoyed making smart-ass comments about how easy it had been to spot. At the same time the CET Commander, Roach, had duly seized Ericka's entire score from the alien wreck on Brahms Three. It would later be impounded back in the CET's presidio in the scavenger town, to be auctioned off for sale. The RGF would get a piece of that action, but Griff was no longer able to line his greasy pockets with an illicit slice of the score. He knew Griff would not forgive him that, but he didn't care. Denying that sadistic bastard his profits was the only satisfaction Hudson could glean from the entire sorry experience.

At least the trip back to Brahms Three had been calm and uneventful. As per RGF regulations, an RGF officer had to accompany any seizure of relics back to the checkpoint district. Ironically, this was in order to confirm that nothing was stolen en route. Griff had traveled back on the CET corvette, with Ericka's repaired freighter following behind, piloted by one of the other CET crew. Ericka's corpse had remained on-board in a body bag. It was now just another item for the coalition authorities to process once they got back to base.

It was only once Hudson was alone in the RGF patrol craft that the full magnitude of what had happened hit him like a bodyslam. He was overcome with anger, grief and guilt, each emotion smashing into him in waves that were unrelenting in their savagery. Eventually, the waves subsided, like a tide going out. However, in their place the stillness of space travel coupled with the void of darkness outside the cockpit left him numb. He had sat in his pilot's chair, simply staring out into space for what ended up being hours. Finally, Hudson's logical mind reasserted itself and told him to pull himself together. *Sitting around moping won't bring her back...* he had told himself. *Don't give in... Don't give Griff the satisfaction of knowing he beat you. Broke you. You have to move on...*

Soon the peace of deep space was replaced by the fiery roar of re-entry through the planet's atmosphere. Before he knew it, Hudson found himself back at the RGF compound, feeling more alone than he'd ever felt in his life.

He finished the shutdown procedures for the RGF patrol craft and opened the rear ramp. The sweaty, pungent heat of Brahms Three flooded the cabin, clinging to his skin like oil. Still numbly operating on autopilot, he stepped outside and logged his arrival into the docking computer. Seismic bass rhythms from one of the nightclubs in the scavenger town vibrated through him. He remained at the computer terminal for a minute or maybe more, feeling the beat resonate in his bones. Each thump was a reminder that his heart was still beating, while Ericka's was not.

Eventually, Hudson headed inside the RGF compound and found the desk sergeant in his usual place, head bowed, reading an epaper. The officer heard Hudson's dragging footsteps and looked up, greeting him with a loud, wide-mouthed yawn.

"Oh, it's you," said the sergeant, once the droning noise coming out of his mouth had subsided. "I don't know what you did, son, but I've never seen discharge orders come through so fast in my life." The sergeant massaged his unshaven face and then lazily slid a datapad across the table towards Hudson.

"Discharge orders?" queried Hudson, walking up to the desk and taking the pad. On it was a memo from Chief Inspector Wash. It began, 'For the attention of the Duty Sergeant, RGF compound, Brahms Three. You are duly notified that Officer Hudson Powell is dismissed from the Relic Guardian Force, for repeated lapses in judgment and gross incompetence in the line of duty. This termination is effective immediately.'

"They can't fire me; I already quit," grumbled Hudson, re-reading the memo to make sure he hadn't missed anything. Hudson had transmitted his resignation letter from the patrol craft, before he'd landed back on Brahms Three.

"No-one ever quits, you should know that," the sergeant replied, sagely. "You try to quit, you get fired. That's how it works."

"But why? What the hell is the point of that?"

"Read on, son, and you'll see..." replied the sergeant, ominously.

Hudson skimmed on to the addendum section and saw what the sergeant was referring to. Wash had deducted Hudson's outstanding relic claim quota for the entire remainder of the year from his pay. This effectively left him with nothing but the hardbucks in his pocket. Not content with this, Hudson's RGF-owned apartment back on Earth was also to be repossessed, and its contents auctioned off to cover his supposed debts. Finally, he noted that the Desk Sergeant was to immediately evict him from his quarters in the RGF compound. Hudson read it all again twice, intermittently laughing at the spitefulness of the language used. However, there was nothing amusing about the fact he was now stranded on Brahms Three, with no way back to Earth. Not that there was anything left for him there now.

"I sure as hell would like to know how you're finding this funny, son," said the desk sergeant in a condescending, fatherly tone. "They just ruined you. Your room has already been cleared. You're out on the street." Then he reached down under his desk and brought up a black plastic bag, which he tossed towards Hudson.

"What's this?" Hudson asked. The sergeant just raised his eyebrows, prompting Hudson to open the bag and peer inside. He was half-expecting a poison cloud to explode in his face, but what he actually found was his civilian clothing, scrunched up into an untidy bundle. "Well, at least you don't kick me out of here naked," he said, more than a little relieved. "That's something, I suppose."

The desk sergeant let out a deep, throaty laugh and then got up out of his chair. "You're not going to give me any trouble, are you, son?" he asked, resting his thumbs inside his belt loops. He smiled and added, "Because I like you. Also, I clock off in ten minutes."

"No, sir, no trouble from me," replied Hudson. He was glad he'd found at least one RGF officer that wasn't a total asshole. "I'll be out of your hair in no time."

The desk sergeant nodded, and then slumped back down in his chair again, "It's a shame, really; the RGF could do with a few more like you. It's just a mob of hotheads and crooks these days, like your lanky friend."

"He's not my friend," snapped Hudson, with far more bite than he'd intended. The image of Ericka's dead body invaded his thoughts again. He forced the memory away, driving it as deeply as he could into the furthest recesses of his conscious mind. He knew it would surface again soon, like a whale coming up for air, but right now he didn't want to feel that pain again. Turning his attention back to the desk sergeant, he added, "Anyway, if you hate the RGF so much, why didn't you quit?" His words were still tainted with bitterness, which meant the question came out almost like an accusation.

"Hell, I'm just too much of a coward, son," replied the desk sergeant. His frankness took Hudson by surprise. "I tried to do things right, back when I was your age, but I just ended up stuck here instead. I figured that's better than what you just got served."

Hudson raised his eyebrows and stared around the decaying halls of the RGF compound. It was just a squalid collection of rusted shipping containers and cheap, fiber-reinforced cement walls. A fat, black rat scurried along the corridor behind the desk sergeant, heading towards the canteen. "You sure about that?"

The desk sergeant laughed and then shot Hudson a crooked smile, "No, I guess not." Then he thrust out his hand, offering it to Hudson, "Good luck, son. I hope you find your way to wherever you need to be."

Hudson took the sergeant's hand and shook it. "Thanks, Sergeant. Me too."

"Call me Larry, I'm not your sergeant anymore."

Hudson nodded, "Okay, Larry. Take care of yourself." Then he turned to leave, but made it only a couple of paces, before a loud, deliberate cough caused him to turn around again.

"You've got to leave that here too, son," said Larry, pointing to Hudson's black and blue uniform, "and your sidearm of course."

"Oh, yeah, sorry," said Hudson, forgetting what he was wearing. He removed his weapon, which Griff had returned to him earlier with an empty clip, and placed it on the desk. Then he went to unbutton his shirt, but was struck by an awkward sense of modesty. "You got somewhere I can change?"

"Well, you ain't allowed back in here, so right there'll have to do," replied Larry. Then he shrugged, and turned his back. "I'll just give you a moment of privacy, son."

Hudson looked around, noticing half a dozen other people within the vicinity of the desk. They were all now staring at him, like he was a window dancer in one of the scavenger town's vice dens. Hudson sighed, before unbuckling his belt and dropping his pants.

CHAPTER 18

Hudson threw back his head and downed his third shot in as many minutes. He let out a contented sigh and placed the glass back onto the counter top with a satisfying thump. Either the flavor of Ma's whiskey was improving or his taste buds were steadily eroding away, much like what was happening to his life. In a matter of hours, he'd gone from being an RGF cop with a steady paycheck and a decent apartment to a broke, homeless nobody. Worse still, he was stranded on a backwater planet with nothing but the clothes on his back and the hardbucks in his pocket, most of which he was frittering away on Ma's whiskey.

"I can't believe he made you get changed in the damn hallway," said Ma, after throwing back another shot of her own. She'd just listened to Hudson's entire sorry story.

Hudson laughed, weakly, "Out of everything I just told you, that's the part you find most surprising?"

Contrary to what he expected, Ma didn't look even the slightest bit amused. In fact, she looked like Hudson had just shot her dog.

"No, that's the *only* part I find surprising," replied Ma, looking unusually serious. "Larry was one of the few good guys, but it looks like the RGF has finally sucked the decency out of him too."

Hudson shrugged, "Larry was alright. He was just doing his job."

Ma re-filled both of their glasses and set the chunky square bottle back down on the counter. "No, he had a choice, same as that pond scum piece of shit, Griff, had a choice." She raised her glass and pointed it at Hudson, "Same as you had a choice about whether to believe Ericka or not, and to help her or not."

Hudson picked up his glass and took a sip, "Yeah, well that didn't work out quite so well did it? For either of us."

"Especially not for her," replied Ma, which drew a pained look from Hudson, but Ma was quick to clarify her comment. "I'm not having a go at you, Hudson, only stating a fact. Truth is, I respect what you did. It took guts, even if it was your pecker doing the thinking, and not your head."

Now Hudson's expression was a mixture of pain and disgust, "Is that what you think? That I helped her because we slept together? Because that's not why I did what I did."

"Why then? Because you loved her?" offered Ma, with a slight raising of her pencil-thin eyebrow.

Hudson necked the rest of the whiskey and thudded the glass back onto the bar, a little harder than he'd intended. He was getting used to the taste again, but he still wasn't immune to its potent after-effects. And one of its byproducts was to strip away the walls he'd erected to box up his feelings.

"I didn't love her, Ma," Hudson replied. He was ashamed and embarrassed to admit it, but it was the truth. "I barely knew her. Sure, I liked her and there was an attraction, so who knows, maybe we could have had something more. But I didn't love her, and I didn't do it for her."

"Then why the hell did you do it?"

"I did it for me," Hudson admitted, again sounding like he was confessing a dirty little secret. "I wanted to 'stick it to the man' and stop them from ripping people off. I hated the way they made me feel; so... dirty and sleazy." Then he shook his head and started to toy with the glass. "So, I bucked authority, and look what it cost." He met Ma's eyes, which were not unsympathetic, yet she was also examining his every word and facial inflection in the way a magistrate might judge a felon. "I don't care about me, Ma, that's not it,"

Hudson added. He didn't need anyone else's judgement; no-one could judge him harder than he'd already judged himself. "But she didn't deserve to die."

Ma sipped her own whiskey and thought for a moment. She had kicked out the regulars of the Landing Strip over an hour earlier and locked the door. However, habit compelled her to check around the bar to make sure no-one else was still lurking, or lying in an alcohol-induced coma under a table. When she was fully satisfied that they were alone, she locked back onto Hudson's eyes. "Would you do it again?"

"What?" asked Hudson, genuinely not sure if he'd heard the question properly due to the mounting effects of the whiskey.

"You said you wanted to stop the RGF from screwing people over," Ma added, trying to re-frame her question in a way that the inebriated former RGF officer might better understand. "If you could roll back the clock, and you were sat here again with Ericka on the other side of the bar, would you try to help her again?" Ma's tone was chilling, serious. "Knowing what you know now."

"I wouldn't want to get her killed again, no," said Hudson, not really following Ma's trajectory of thought. "What the hell kind of question is that?"

"Look, Hudson, here's how I see it," Ma went on, "You rushed out of here to help her on gut instinct. And if you're being truthful with me about thinking with your head and not your..." Hudson coughed loudly, "your you-know-what..." said Ma, which was about as subtle as she ever got, "and that you stood to gain nothing from it, other than a fine sense of wellbeing for helping out a stranger, I don't believe you did it for yourself. You did it because it was the right thing to do."

"Jeez, Ma, if you're going to hit me with this sort of deep psychoanalysis, you could at least pull up a couch for me to lie on. Or pour me another."

Ma smiled and obliged by refilling both of their glasses. Then she pointed a manicured finger at Hudson as if she was about to make another incisive observation. "You know what I really think?"

"Hit me..." said Hudson, sipping the whiskey.

"I think you're a good man, Hudson Powell," said Ma, enthusiastically.

Hudson smiled and raised his tumbler, which Ma met with her own. There was a crisp chink of crystal glass and then both of them drained the contents in perfect synchronization. "Thanks, Ma," said Hudson, genuinely. "But, it seems the world doesn't care about good guys. The truth is, good guys get people killed, and end up with nothing, while the bastards from the RGF get away with murder."

Ma reached down underneath the counter and returned with two objects. One was a little pill box, and the other was a black carton, about the size of a cigarette packet. She slid both towards Hudson and then looked at him expectantly.

"What are these?" asked Hudson frowning at each item in turn.

Ma tapped her finger on the black cigarette packet-sized carton first. "This little gadget got me out of a fair few scrapes when I was a relic hunter," she began, as if reminiscing the good old days. "It's a skelly; something that will help you get into places you shouldn't be."

"A skelly? You mean a skeleton key?" queried Hudson, picking up the device and turning it over in his hands. He blew out a long, low whistle. "You do realize these things are highly illegal, even in the Outer Portal Worlds."

"Relic hunting is a complicated business," replied Ma, with a little extra verve. "It's old, and many of the portal worlds have upgraded their encryption since I last used it, so in most places it's obsolete." Then she smiled, showing her perfect white teeth. "Most places, but not here."

Hudson's eyes widened. "What can it open?"

Ma shrugged, "Pretty much any door in the scavenger town, apart from mine of course. Plus, the RGF compound, the back door to the CET's barracks, and, oh... the vaults too."

Hudson laughed at the accidently-on-purpose way Ma had highlighted the skelly's ability to open the vaults. "The vaults, huh?" he said, playing it coy.

"Yeah, you know, just in case there was something in there that someone might want to get back," continued Ma, matching Hudson's cloak-and-dagger tone. Then she ruined the act with her characteristic lack of subtlety. "As in, get back a certain somebody's score and then pass it along to her brother."

"I got it, Ma," said Hudson, smiling broadly, before placing the skelly back on the counter. "What's the rush, though? I'm quite enjoying drowning my sorrows."

Ma shook her head, "For an RGF cop, you sure as shit don't know much about seized relic claims."

"What can I say, I'm a lousy cop," said Hudson, with a short shrug.

"They will clear those vaults at second sunrise and ship the contents to the auction house. So, if you're not in there tonight, your chance is shot."

"Right, good point," Hudson replied, nodding in agreement. He quickly regretted moving his head so sharply, as his pickled brain seemed to continue swaying. "I'm hardly in any condition to go on a heist though, am I? Drunk criminals tend to get caught."

Ma tapped the second, smaller box on the table, and Hudson turned his attention to it. "And what's this?"

Ma snapped opened the box to reveal two small capsules. "These are nanolivers."

"No way, I've heard of these, but never seen them for real," said Hudson, marveling at the little capsules. They were even rarer than the skelly. "Do they actually work?"

"Yes, they do," replied Ma. "These things have gotten me out of as many scrapes as that skelly. And you're right that you'll need sobering up if you're going to rob the vault tonight."

Hudson closed the lid of the nanoliver box and looked at Ma with more sober eyes. He couldn't deny that the idea of stealing back Ericka's score was appealing. If he could still help her brother, it would certainly go some way towards appeasing his own guilt. However, he wasn't quite drunk enough to believe that a skelly and a clear head was all he needed to pull it off. "Thanks, Ma, but even if I did manage to break into the vaults, I'd never get off Brahms Three." He rocked back on his stool and pointed to his pockets. "Everything I had left, I just spent filling my bloodstream with a chemical that those little pills will render inert."

"I'll shout you a ticket back to Earth," said Ma, and Hudson nearly fell backwards off his stool.

"Ma, I appreciate all of this, I really do, but I can't pay you back for any of it," admitted Hudson. "I can barely pay you for the whiskey."

Ma waved a hand at him, "I don't want your money, Hudson."

"Then why?"

"I told you, because you're a good guy," replied Ma with earnest. "Besides, you're broke and homeless, and you sure as hell aren't staying here tonight. So, it's the only way I'm going to get rid of your sorry ass."

"And here's me thinking I still had my charm to rely on," replied Hudson, with a smirk.

"Oh, you're charming enough, Hudson Powell, but also not my type," Ma replied, with an even more wicked smirk.

"Oh, and what's your type then?"

"*Not* broke, jobless and homeless," replied Ma, straight faced.

"Ouch..." said Hudson, "but, also, fair point."

"There's a transport leaving in the morning, at first sunrise," said Ma. "It's fully booked, but the skipper's an old flame of mine from back in the day. He'll let you on-board if you mention my name, and leave him a little something to sweeten the deal."

"You old dog!" said Hudson flashing her a feigned look of shocked surprise. "And here I was thinking I'm the charmer."

"You just make sure your bony ass is on that transport in the morning," Ma answered, turning a little red in the cheek. She then re-filled both of their glasses, emptying the bottle of whiskey in the process. "Now, let's have another drink to seal the bargain, before you sober up."

"To daring deeds," said Hudson, raising his glass.

"To doing the right thing," said Ma, chinking Hudson's glass. Then both of them drank the contents in one gulp. "Now, go on, before I change my mind."

Hudson opened the box, placed the nanolivers in his mouth and swallowed them. Then he stuffed the skelly in his jacket pocket and slid off the stool. The nanolivers had yet to kick in, and so he had to hold onto the edge of the bar to steady himself. His head was spinning like a whirling dervish.

"I meant what I said the first time you rocked up in here," said Ma, wiping the counter top down with a yellow rag.

"Which bit? That I'm honest, but not too bright?"

"Well, that too," said Ma, evidently having forgotten that she'd said that as well. "But, no. I meant when I said you'd make a good relic hunter. If you manage to get off this rock alive, give it some thought. It's a hell of lot more fun than flying courier runs."

"I'll think about it," said Hudson, though in truth, the idea hadn't been far from his mind for some time. Then he turned to leave, feeling the effects of the nanolivers finally start to take hold. He reached the door and waited for Ma to buzz the lock, before pushing it open. A wave of cloying, sticky heat washed in from the street outside. Hudson paused and looked back at Ma for a final time. "Thanks, Ma. Whether you like it or not, I owe you one."

"Several, I'd reckon," replied Ma, standing with her hands pressed to her toned hips. "But you're welcome, Hudson Powell. Now, go stick it to 'em."

Hudson shot her a little salute, then slipped out into the musky night air, clear-headed and filled with a renewed sense of purpose.

CHAPTER 19

The nanolivers worked fast, which Hudson soon came to realize was both a blessing and a curse. On the one hand, he was back in full command of his enviable pilot's reflexes. Yet on the other, sobriety had opened his eyes fully to the stark stupidity of what he'd drunkenly agreed to do. He considered timidly knocking on the door of the Landing Strip to ask Ma if she actually had some semblance of an idea about how to pull off this little stunt. However, the idea of crawling back with his tail between his legs was too humiliating. He'd already lost enough; he didn't want to risk losing Ma's respect and admiration too.

Instead, he pressed his hands into his pockets and ambled off towards the CET presidio, where the vaults were located. In addition to giving the nanolivers time to work, the walk also let him run through various scenarios in his mind. It helped that he knew Brahms Three pretty well. And it also helped that compared to the scavenger towns on the near-Earth portal worlds, security on Brahms Three was hardly at the gold standard. Yet it was also true that trying to break into a CET vault was a good way of getting yourself killed. The skelly gave him an advantage, for sure. However, before he could unlock the vault, he first had to get inside the presidio. Any sensible outlaw would spend a week planning such a bold heist. Hudson had only until first sunrise to get in, out, and off world again.

He reached the perimeter fence that cordoned off the small CET presidio from the rest of the scavenger town, and leant up against the side wall of a seedy-looking bar. He was still fruitlessly wracking his brains for a way to get inside undetected. Despite it being the dead of night, there were still plenty of people milling around. It was the usual mix of street walkers and night-time pleasure seekers that Brahms Three had evolved to serve so well.

No-one paid Hudson any attention, until one of the women who had been loitering outside the bar sidled up to him. She casually leant back against the wall, crossed one long leg in front of the other and then shot him a glance. Hudson knew it was intended to look spontaneous, but it was merely part of a thoroughly practiced act. This wasn't the first time Hudson had been propositioned, and he was quick to head her off.

"Before you ask, I'm not interested," he said, trying to sound as friendly as possible. However, the fierce scowl he was met with in return seemed to suggest he'd failed miserably.

"Well, what the bloody hell are you doing skulking around out here then?" snapped the woman. "This is hardly a spot for sightseeing, love."

Hudson smiled; she had a point. He couldn't think of any good reason why he was there, which was because his reason for being there wasn't good. "I'm thinking about how to break into the presidio and rob it," said Hudson, deciding that telling the truth would sound just as unbelievable as any lie he could come up with on the spot.

"Oh yeah?" said the woman, seemingly playing along with Hudson's game. "How'd you plan to do that then?"

Hudson shrugged, "I have absolutely no idea. I don't suppose you have any suggestions?"

This seemed to amuse the woman. She teased a flattened cigarette out of a pocket inside her tight denim shorts, and placed it delicately in her mouth. "That makes you a bit of a shit robber then, doesn't it?" she said, before pointing to the cigarette. "Got a light?"

"Sorry, I don't smoke," replied Hudson. He realized this was probably a good thing, since only minutes earlier there had been so much alcohol in his blood that the spark of a lighter would have sent him up like a firework.

The woman tutted obviously. "Bloody hell, you're just about the most useless tosser I've met tonight, and that's saying something."

Hudson scowled back at her, but then his attention was distracted by a man in a CET uniform who was walking towards them. He was young, perhaps in his early twenties, and he looked like he'd only woken up five minutes ago. The name badge on his shirt read, 'Private Hanes'.

Hanes glanced briefly at the woman, before sheepishly addressing Hudson. "Uh, are you her pimp?"

"Piss off, we're all freelance here," the woman shot back, before Hudson had a chance to speak. "Pimp indeed. This isn't the movies, love. Got a light?"

The soldier fumbled around in his many pockets and eventually found a cheap-looking plastic lighter. He leant over and used it to ignite the woman's cigarette.

"So, what's the deal then?" Hanes said, placing the lighter into a different pocket to the one he'd found it in. "Are you already, uh, taken?" He glanced at Hudson as he said this.

"No, he's planning to break into the presidio and rob it, so I'm all yours," said the woman without even a hint of sarcasm. She smiled and then blew out a narrow column of smoke directly in the soldier's face.

Hudson felt like his heart literally jumped into his throat. He kept his cool and glanced up at the private, before shoving his hands into his pockets and nodding, "Looks like I'm busted."

There was an awkward silence while the heavy-eyed private processed both responses. Then he blurted out a crude, chesty laugh and pointed at Hudson with a broad smile on his face. "You guys, you almost had me there!" he continued, spittle launching from his mouth as he tried to control his laughter. "I'm on duty in there in about thirty minutes, so you best not try anything!" he added by way of a mock warning.

"You're a guard in the presidio?" said Hudson, trying not to sound too interested by the soldier's revelation.

"Yeah, for the next twelve *long* hours, man," the private replied, making it sound as if it he'd been sentenced to twenty years hard labor. "So, I thought I'd get a little pick me up first, you know?"

"Oh, totally," said Hudson, which was a lie, but he was eager to encourage the young private on. "You'd best get a move on though, if you're on duty in half an hour."

"Hey, stop trying to pimp me out," said the woman, rapping Hudson playfully on the shoulder with the back of her hand. She then turned back to Private Hanes and sucked another long drag on the cigarette, which was already almost burned out. She blew the smoke into his face again and said, "So, what's it to be, Private?"

"Lead the way!" said Hanes, with an even broader grin. He then winked at Hudson and followed the woman back along the road in front of the bar.

Hudson waved as the clearly ecstatic Private Hanes practically skipped up a metal flight of stairs in pursuit of the street walker. The stairs led into a row of converted shipping containers stacked above the bar. He observed them with the detailed scrutiny of a private detective and saw the woman reach into her denim shorts and pull out a keycard. She then pressed the card to the lock, before pushing open the door and stepping inside. Private Hanes wasted no time in rushing in behind.

"It can't be that easy, can it?" wondered Hudson, feeling inside his jacket pocket for the skelly. Then he again looked up at the door at the top of the metal stairwell. "Surely, it can't be that simple?"

He mulled the idea over in his mind for a couple of minutes. This was as much to allow Private Hanes time to get his uniform off, since he'd be needing it himself. Then he committed to the act, and started to casually walk towards the stairwell with the skelly held firmly in his right hand. He wasn't proud of what he was about to do. And he certainly had no desire to witness the scene that was inevitably already unfolding behind the locked door. Yet he also knew it was perhaps the only chance he had of getting inside the presidio, without getting killed.

"Sorry, Private," Hudson muttered under his breath as he held the skelly up next to the lock. Lights on the device immediately began to flash as it decoded the security key. "But I'm afraid tonight isn't going to go down quite as you'd planned..."

CHAPTER 20

Hudson marched towards the CET Presidio wearing the uniform formerly belonging to Private Hanes. The act of acquiring the uniform had not been one of the finer moments in the life of Hudson Powell esquire. Remarkably, though, unlike many of his other schemes, the plan had actually worked out well. After bursting through the door, he'd literally caught Hanes with his pants down. And as the young soldier stood there, stark, bollock naked with his mouth agape and dignity laid bare, it hadn't taken much for Hudson to sucker-punch him to the floor.

The woman, whose name still remained a mystery, was also more than a little pissed off at the interruption. However, she had soon calmed down after Hudson wafted a stack of hardbucks in her face. This was the money Ma had fortunately decided not to charge him for all the whiskey he'd drunk, and then nullified with the nanolivers. The woman had even helped to tie Hanes up and gag him, on the promise that Hudson would give her a cut of whatever he managed to steal from the vaults in the presidio. It was actually this lie, more than the act of denying Private Hanes his clothes and a fumble beneath the sheets, that he felt most guilty about.

Private Hanes had been a little leaner than Hudson, but on the whole the uniform fitted remarkably well. In fact, he couldn't believe his luck. Had Hanes been a hundred pounds heavier or five inches shorter, this hair-brained scheme of his couldn't have worked. For once it seemed like the cards were falling in Hudson's favor. He'd even acquired a genuine security keycard, which had enabled him to enter the presidio through a side gate without raising suspicion. However, as he headed towards the main complex, amazed at his continued good fortune, he spotted another soldier marching towards him. Hudson took several deep breaths and prepared himself, hoping that this guard, like Hanes, lacked Logan Griff's talent for seeing through bullshit.

"Are you my relief?" snapped the guard, whose name badge read, 'Private Yardley'. He looked even younger than Private Hanes and spoke with a nasally voice that immediately got on Hudson's nerves.

"Yeah, that's me," said Hudson, trying to mimic Hanes' jocular tone. "I'm Private Hanes."

"Well, yeah, I can see that," said Yardley, pointing to the name badge on Hudson's shirt. "You must be new around here, Hanes, because we change-over five minutes in advance of the scheduled hour. You're already ten minutes late!" Yardley's adenoidal voice rose in pitch with each sentence, so that by the end of his tirade only dogs could have heard him properly.

"Yeah, sorry, I'll know for next time," said Hudson, not really knowing what else to say.

"Whatever, man, I'm late already," Yardley went on, while unclipping a carabiner from his belt loop and shoving a bunch of keycards into Hudson's hand. "These are the keys to the base. Oh, and it's just you on duty in this section tonight. Richards called in sick again, the skiving asshole. So, if you need anything, just radio the guards in the tower."

"Hey, no problem," said Hudson using his 'Hanes voice' again. Once again, he could hardly believe his luck. He saluted and added, "You take it easy man."

Yardley grumbled an indistinct reply and then marched off towards the main exit. Hudson was left alone in the yard, feeling more than a little shell shocked. He checked his watch and saw that first sunrise was three hours away. He still had enough time to get inside the vault, assuming the skelly was able to work its magic.

Hudson walked up to the door of the main block, and then cycled through the various keyfobs that Yardley had thrust upon him. Eventually, he found the one that opened the door, and stepped inside. He was vaguely familiar with the layout of CET presidios like this one, having done courier runs to many of them in the past. However, he'd never seen the vaults, and so had no choice but to wander the halls, hoping to get lucky. After a few anxious wrong turns, dead ends and nervous checks of his watch, he eventually found the vault room. Frantically, he cycled through each of the keycards, but none opened the door.

"Figures..." Hudson muttered out loud, "I wouldn't trust this bunch of airhead guards with the keys to the vault room either." He clipped the keycards to his belt and pulled the skelly out of his jacket pocket. "Luckily, I have my own key..." he added, still muttering under his breath, before switching on the device and pressing it to the lock. The skelly clamped on magnetically and green LEDs began to flash as it decrypted the entry code.

Compared to the lock to the boudoir that he'd 'picked' earlier, the locking mechanism for the vault room was far more sophisticated, and progress was painfully slow. Hudson hoped that Ma had been right about the security systems on Brahms Three being outdated, because if the skelly didn't work, he was sunk.

Time ticked on as Hudson waited impatiently for the skelly to finish. It was the early hours of the morning and the presidio was so deathly quiet that Hudson thought he could have heard a gnat fart. As the skelly worked, occasionally bleeping and chirping softly, every little noise felt like a firecracker going off next to his ear. After one of the most nerve-wracking four and a half minutes of his life, the skelly finally decrypted the lock. He pulled the device away from the keypad and slipped inside the vault room, closing the door behind him with the gentleness of a teenager sneaking home from a curfew-breaking night out on the town.

Wasting no time, Hudson crept up to the vault door and attached the skelly to the lock. Given that it had taken almost five minutes to crack the door to the vault room, Hudson expected a much longer wait to open the vault door itself. He slid the switch to activate the device and then huddled down to wait. The green LEDs flickered chaotically as the device probed the lock mechanism to reveal its secrets.

Several minutes ticked by, during which time Hudson's heart-rate had fallen to an almost normal level. Then he heard footsteps outside and his blood pressure rocketed again. He crept back to the door, pulse racing, and listened. There were heavy boots clomping along the polished stone floor of the hallway directly outside.

Damn it, the second guard has come on duty! Hudson thought, and he began to frantically scan the vault room for places to hide or escape. However, the room was empty, bar a couple of metal-framed tables that wouldn't even hide a mouse. The door he'd entered through was also the only way in or out. Any attempt to leave would place him directly in the path of whomever was approaching.

Shit! he cursed, as he pressed his body flat against the wall directly beside the door. This was the only location where he could hide from the gaze of anyone who peered through the glass. If he was lucky, the other guard would just breeze past the vault room or take a casual peek inside and then move on. If his luck had finally run out then he'd have to improvise. *Hell, I've already assaulted one CET soldier tonight, so adding another to the rap sheet won't make much of a difference...* he figured.

The footsteps grew louder and then seemed to stop. Hudson held his breath, careful not to make even the slightest sound. Then he heard the door to the vault room gently creak open. The shadowy outline of a man crept inside and took two careful paces into the room. The figure was still shielded from Hudson by the open door, and he didn't want to risk a move until he had a clear run at whoever it was. Yet for some reason the man hung back. Hudson felt like his lungs were going to burst, willing the guard to take another step forward. Then he noticed that the guard's gaze appeared to be directed at the vault door. Hudson glanced over and saw the flashing green lights of the skelly, still working to crack the lock's encryption. He cursed himself for leaving it in plain sight. If the guard had spotted the skelly then he'd charge out of the room at any moment to raise the alarm. Hudson knew he'd run out of options and out of time; he had no choice but to act.

Barging his shoulder into the open door, Hudson launched the guard into the vault room, as if he'd been hit by a rampaging bull. The guard tumbled and skidded across the shiny floor, arms and legs flailing helplessly. Hudson rushed over, conscious of ensuring the guard didn't get chance to cry out for help. Hudson slid down at the guard's side and pressed his hand over the man's mouth, feeling a wiry mustache push back against his skin. Hudson then drew back a fist, ready to strike, before he saw the man's eyes cleanly for the first time and froze. It wasn't a CET guard. The man was Logan Griff.

CHAPTER 21

Hudson's moment of startled indecision was all that Griff needed to throw him aside. Hudson slid across the polished floor and clambered to his feet, before squaring off against Griff. However, his former training officer had already expertly drawn his sidearm and was aiming it at Hudson's chest. In a split second, the tables had turned.

"What the hell are you doing here, rook?" yelled Griff. He wiped his mouth on his shirt sleeve to remove the sweaty imprint of Hudson's hand. Griff then he noticed the skelly again and a smug grin lit up his face. "You're here to rob the vault? And with a skelly too; I'm actually impressed." Griff let out a mocking laugh. "And to think I actually believed all your crap about doing things 'by the book'. Truth is you're no different to me."

"I'm nothing like you!" Hudson spat back. "You only think about yourself. I'm not stealing this stuff for me. I made a promise, and I intend to keep it."

Griff's eyes narrowed and he shook his head. "This here is the only person that matters, rook," he said, tapping himself on the chest with a yellowed finger. "Looking out for number one is why I keep beating you. But I guess that's a lesson you'll never learn."

"So why are you in here, big shot?" Hudson hit back. "Robbing a vault seems a bit desperate, even for you."

"Yeah, well some moron went and cost me my score, remember?" Griff growled. His mood had soured just as quickly as he'd drawn his sidearm. "And now Wash is on my ass to pay your full outstanding quota as well as mine. And I don't have that kind of money."

"Why my quota too?" asked Hudson. He was trying to stall Griff and buy time to think, but he was genuinely curious too.

"Payback for Wash backing up my story with the CET. Those stiff assholes wanted to open an investigation into your girlfriend's death."

Hudson flushed with anger, but managed to hold himself back, "Don't talk about her, you murdering bastard," he growled, jabbing a finger at Griff like it was the tip of a knife.

"Or what, rook?" Griff hit back. He had seemed to find Hudson's threat more insulting than intimidating. "You already screwed up your chance to take me down. You should have left Brahms Three while you had the chance."

"Yeah, well thanks to you, the RGF left me with nothing, so it's not like I had a choice."

"You had a choice," replied Griff. Hudson could almost taste the bitterness in his breath. "You chose to double-cross me, and now it's going to cost you, like I promised it would."

There was a quiet trio of beeps from behind them as the skelly finished deciphering the vault key. This was followed by a resonant thud as the bolts holding the thick steel door shut retracted into their housing.

"After you, rook," said Griff, motioning for Hudson to back towards the vault with the barrel of his pistol. Hudson now noticed the weapon had a suppressor attached. "Thanks for saving me the effort of breaking it open." Then he seemed to have an epiphany and his face scrunched into a confused scowl. "I had to bribe a night guard to give me his keyfobs and take a sick day, so how did you get in here? And where did you get a skelly; you just said you were broke?"

"Maybe I'm smarter than you think, after all," said Hudson, being deliberately evasive. He was conscious of not saying anything that might implicate Ma and put her or the Landing Strip onto Griff's radar. Ericka had paid the ultimate price for getting involved with him, and Hudson's fragile conscience couldn't stand it if Ma got hurt too.

Griff shrugged and then tapped the weapon with his free hand, "Not quite smart enough, though." Then he redirected the barrel of the weapon towards the circular door behind Hudson, "Now, open the vault, step inside and head to the back."

Hudson felt a chill shoot down his spine. "Why, what are you going to do?" Every instinct warned him that getting inside the vault was a bad idea.

"You're going to rob it for me," said Griff, casually. "It's the least you can do for all the trouble you've caused."

"And then what?"

"And then you're going to be my fall guy, of course. The CET will open the door at second sunrise and find you inside. You're a ready-made scapegoat." Griff shrugged again, "Assuming you don't suffocate and die first, but then I don't give a shit either way. Point is, they'll arrest you and won't be looking for me." He aimed his weapon at Hudson's right leg, "Now, open the door and get inside, before I put a bullet into your foot. That would make your stay in 'vault city' a whole lot less comfortable, don't you think?"

Hudson did as he was instructed, hauling the heavy vault door open before stepping over the threshold. He knew that his prospects of getting out alive were deteriorating rapidly, but he didn't see that he had a choice. Griff wasn't bluffing about locking him inside the vault. And Hudson also believed that he'd wound him to prove his point if provoked. However, he didn't believe for a second that Griff would leave him alive. He must have known that Hudson would implicate him as an accomplice. He was merely dangling the prospect of survival as a way to gain Hudson's co-operation. Griff had already threatened to kill him once in order to silence him, and there was no reason to believe this situation would be any different. Hudson had to stop Griff, before he'd had his fill from the vault, otherwise he was dead. However, time was running out.

Griff followed Hudson inside, removing his flattened, empty backpack before throwing it at Hudson's feet. "Start filling that up, rook," he commanded, "and only with the good stuff. I'll be watching, so don't try anything stupid, if that's even possible for you."

"Don't you ever get bored of ripping people off?" said Hudson. He opened the bag and began rifling through the contents of the vault's shelves, placing some of the more valuable alien relics inside. His only chance now was to find something in the vault he could use against Griff. It was a long shot, but he'd had more good luck than bad so far today. He had to believe he could still roll a hard six.

"Don't you ever get tired of pissing me off?" replied Griff, vindictively. "Just shut the hell up and fill the bag. And be on the lookout for something that looks like a crystal, about the length of a hand with a weird metallic sheen. Maybe the girl got lucky and found it."

The crystal again? thought Hudson, wondering what was so important about this new discovery to warrant so much attention. He played dumb, and tried to eke out some more information from Griff. "I've never heard of a crystal being found on a wreck. What does it do?"

"How the hell should I know?" replied Griff, irritably. "But any new relic discovery could be worth a fortune." Then he scowled and raised his weapon a little higher. "You sure you don't know anything about a crystal? That would actually explain why you and the lady hooked up."

"I didn't help Ericka for money," said Hudson, resentful that Griff would assume he could sink to his level. "Her brother is broke and about to lose his home, his kids... everything."

Griff bellowed out a laugh, "And you bought that crap? Man, you are a special case, aren't you?"

"I wouldn't expect you to understand," said Griff, tossing a few more alien components into the bag. "You only care about 'number one' right?"

"You expect me to believe you'd risk your own life to rob this place just out of sentiment?" spat Griff, his contempt growing more apparent with each word that passed his lips. "Fulfilling her dying wish, is that really it?" He laughed again.

Hudson threw down the piece of alien tech in his hand and made a move towards Griff, but the muted crack of his suppressed sidearm made him stop dead. Hudson frantically checked himself, expecting to see blood leaking from a wound, but he wasn't injured.

"That was a warning – the only one you'll get. The next one goes into your gut, rook," warned Griff. "I'll fill the damn bag myself if I have to."

Hudson backed away and then returned to scouring the shelves, his heart thumping. He'd let Griff rile him, and he was lucky to still be alive. Now, with the bag almost full, he perhaps only had another minute or two to come up with something – anything – to take Griff down first.

Then Hudson spotted something familiar that had gotten pushed to the back of a shelf. He glanced across to Griff, who was yawning and no longer paying close attention, and took a more detailed look. *Ericka's electroshock ring?* Thought Hudson, unsure if he was remembering it correctly. It certainly looked like the device she'd used to subdue the mugger in the alleyway. Checking again to make sure Griff wasn't watching, he casually slipped the ring onto his finger. If it was the electroshock ring, it might just end up saving his life, just as it had saved Ericka. And if it wasn't then he was going to look as dumb as Griff already thought he was, except a whole lot deader.

189

"Come on, rook, I don't have all night," complained Griff, again prodding the weapon in Hudson's direction.

The mention of time seemed to make him more anxious. Like Hudson, Griff would have known that the CET cleared the vault at second sunrise. Griff stepped back over the threshold to check the coast was still clear outside. Hudson used the opportunity to stuff the bag with a couple of larger, less valuable items. It was enough to make it look like he'd done his job. He pulled the drawstring of the rucksack and then clipped the flap shut, before holding the bag out towards Griff.

"Here's your blood money," Hudson called over. He was intentionally teasing the bag in front of his body in order to entice Griff closer. He doubted that his former partner would risk shooting him with the bag full of relics held up like a shield. "Murder, extortion, theft... I wonder how you sleep at night?"

Griff stepped back inside the vault and eyed the bag, greedily. "I sleep just fine, rook. Now, throw the bag over."

Hudson took a measured pace forward. "You want me to throw a bag full of fragile alien tech at you?" he said, in an 'are you really that stupid' tone of voice.

Griff took another step closer, but still left a good couple of meters between him and Hudson. "Just put it down and then back off," he snarled, again jabbing the barrel of the weapon towards him.

"Did you ever play sports?" asked Hudson.

"What?" replied Griff. The question had briefly thrown him.

"Sports, did you ever play?" Hudson repeated.

"No. What kind of asinine question is that?"

"I just wanted to know if you can catch..." said Hudson. And as he spoke the word 'catch', he threw the bag at Griff. Hudson watched as Griff's gaunt, mustachioed face contorted and eyes widened, tracking the rucksack as it arced towards him like a football. Instinctively, Griff went to seize the bag before it crashed to the solid metal floor. Both hands stretched out for it as if he was about to take a match-winning catch. However, before Griff's arms could close fully around the tough, black fabric, Hudson rushed forward and drove a shoulder into his bony ribs. If it had been a football match, Hudson would have made the perfect play. As soon as Griff's back hit the floor, Hudson reached up and pressed the electroshock ring against his neck, holding it firmly against his mottled skin. Griff spasmed and convulsed like a dancing Halloween skeleton. Enjoying Griff's pain perhaps a little more than he should, Hudson finally released the pressure and rolled aside. His own body was fizzing with adrenalin and residual shock from being in contact with Griff while the ring discharged.

191

Hudson lay on his back for a minute or two in order to recover his breath and stop himself from shaking. Then he pushed himself to his feet and stared down at Griff. He was out cold, with an ugly burn mark smoldering on his neck, like a love bite gone horribly wrong.

Hudson blew out a heavy sigh and then said, triumphantly, "Touchdown, asshole."

CHAPTER 22

Hudson checked the time; first sunrise was a little under two Earth hours away. This was just enough time to grab some valuable relics and get to the transport. With Logan Griff still unconscious on the floor, Hudson set about scouring the vault for the choicest items to steal. Griff's rucksack was too large and conspicuous, and the unregistered contents would still set off the Shaak radiation alarms. Every scavenger town had a very limited black-market trade in alien artefacts, but he didn't have time to auction them on Brahms Three. In order to get off the planet without raising suspicion, he'd need something subtle; something he could find a way of hiding from the Shaak scanners.

Hudson frantically searched the vault for something small and highly valuable. He then caught sight of what looked like a brown leather satchel, shoved into the far corner. He went over to check it, but as he picked it up, he realized that it wasn't a satchel, but a jacket. He recognized it immediately as Ericka's over-sized leather jacket. There was a bullet hole just above the left pocket, and Ericka's blood was still visible.

Hudson pressed his eyes shut and dropped to his knees, gripping the jacket as if it were a long-lost childhood teddy bear. Her death again played out in his mind, no matter how hard he tried not to see. The stab of guilt was powerful and unexpected. He thought he'd managed to bury his feelings, and was unprepared for how quickly and potently they had reemerged. "I'm sorry, Ericka..." he said out loud, though speaking the words didn't make him feel any better.

The constraints of time soon compelled him to get moving again. Wondering why the CET would bother to add the jacket to the vault at all, he checked the area around where he'd found it. There were several other items in the same location and a sign that said, 'Incident 00F-1A (Case Closed) - Evidence to incinerate.' Hudson released a heavy sigh, "Evidence to incinerate..." he spoke out loud, shaking his head. Then his mind went to a darker place, wondering what had become of Ericka's body.

He stood up and removed the CET military jacket belonging to Private Hanes, tossing it into the pile of other items marked for incineration. He then pulled on Ericka's leather jacket, and smiled as he discovered that it fitted perfectly. It had been way too big for her, perhaps intentionally to mask weapons or otherwise just allow her to carry more on her person. However, on Hudson it looked like it had been tailored precisely to his measurements.

Hudson pressed his hands into the pockets and found a small clip of hardbucks. He took it out and counted it; five hundred and thirty in total. Not much, but he was amazed the clip was still there at all. *Obviously, the CET have more of a moral code than the bastards at the RGF*, Hudson supposed. Then he felt something pressing into his chest and slipped his hand inside, discovering the concealed compartment that Ericka had shown him in the alley. The strange metallic, crystal was still there. He slid it out and held it in his hands, again transfixed by its mesmerizing alien sheen. "Well, you are certainly creating a lot of attention," he said to the crystal, as if it could hear him. "I wonder what you are..." He slipped the crystal back into the compartment and smiled. He had an idea.

He recalled how Ericka had explained that the lining of the pocket acted as a shield against the alien radiation signature. He knew he wouldn't be able to fit much inside the compartment, alongside the mysterious crystal. However, if he selected only the highest value items, it still might be enough to pay off Ericka's brother's debts.

Checking the time again and noting how little he had left, he moved through the vault, rummaging through drawers and shelving racks. He needed just three or four relics that would fetch a good price at auction. Then he saw what he needed; a collection of high-grade CPU shards. These were small enough to fit in the hidden compartment, but rare enough to fetch a high price at auction.

Along with other alien computer tech, these were amongst the best scores on any relic hunt. Small, light and highly valuable, the high-grade shards were prized by the military for their intelligent processing capabilities. It had taken a decade for the scientists on Earth to figure out the technology used in the shards. The secrets gleaned from them had been responsible for the rapid development of more sophisticated spaceships and installations. Yet, the exotic alien materials and processes used meant that it had still been impossible to recreate the high-grade shards fully. As such, the MP and CET militaries paid top dollar for intact high-grade components.

He slipped the alien computing devices into the pocket alongside the crystal and then ran back to the vault door. He'd almost forgotten that Griff was still lying in front of it. Except he was no longer out cold, but beginning to stir.

Hudson spotted Griff's sidearm, next to the wall of the vault and picked it up. For a split second he considered aiming the pistol at Griff and pulling the trigger. *He has it coming...* Hudson thought. *It's natural justice!* Griff was more than just a loathsome individual; he was a cold-blooded murderer, who would come for Hudson again, if left alive. Then he remembered what he'd said to Tory Bellona, inside the alien wreck. If he shot Griff, he'd be no better than he was.

Griff groaned and groggily sat upright, before he spotted Hudson, weapon in hand and froze. However, the shock was only short-lived, and soon Griff's pained grimace morphed into a condescending, smug smirk.

"You won't do it, rook," he said, rubbing his neck and wincing. "You don't have the guts."

Hudson raised the weapon and aimed it at Griff's head, finger on the trigger. "It's nothing more than you deserve. Why should I let you live, after what you've done?"

"You shouldn't," said Griff, without delay. "If you were smart, you'd have already pulled that trigger, but you won't. You're weak, and you know it."

Hudson shook his head, and slid his finger off the trigger. "You're wrong," he snarled back at him. "You have no idea how much strength is needed for me not to end your sorry existence right now."

"See, I told you," Griff laughed, "So long as you're too gutless to do what needs to be done, I'll always beat you, rook."

"Death is too good for you, Griff," said Hudson, easing off and stepping back over the threshold of the vault door. "You can stay here and wait for the CET instead. A decade in a max security prison station should suit you nicely; plenty of other vermin to mix with."

Griff tried to stand, but he grimaced and groaned in pain, before collapsing to his knees. "You might walk away this time," Griff said, panting from the pain and exertion, "but I'll find you. I'm going to make you my special project, Hudson Powell. There's nowhere you can go that I won't find you."

"Then I guess I'll see you out there," said Hudson. "Enjoy your time in jail."

Hudson stepped outside the vault and closed the heavy metal door. He then plucked the skelly off the lock and shoved it into the pocket of his new leather jacket. There was a resonant thud as the bolts slammed into place, sealing the door shut, with Griff still inside. Hudson knew that the CET shift change would happen before the oxygen in the vault ran out; another mercy that Griff didn't deserve. As much as he wanted rid of Griff, he wouldn't sink to his level. He might not have had a book to go by anymore, but he still had a code. And he still had his honor.

Hudson crept out of the vault room and carefully made his way back through the corridors of the presidio. It was still as empty and deathly quiet as when he'd first entered. Yet, in less than two hours, the base would be humming with activity. He wondered what explanation Griff would give to the guards when they found him, and whether Chief Inspector Wash would once again come to his aid and back him up. This time, Hudson didn't think so. With any luck, Wash would throw Griff to the wolves, and he'd end up in a dark cell, in a dark part of the galaxy.

Even if Griff did manage to slime and wheedle his way out of a long stint in prison, Hudson wasn't afraid. Griff's threat of making him his 'special project' didn't faze him in the slightest. He wasn't going to live in fear. He'd show Griff that he was the better man, and frustrate the asshole's every attempt to beat him. Griff's punishment would be to see Hudson succeed.

Hudson slipped outside into the CET compound. It was already getting lighter; first sunrise would be soon and he had to get out fast. Moving swiftly and silently, he used his assortment of keyfobs to open a side-access gate and slipped out into the scavenger town unseen. The space port was about ten minutes away, at a fast jog. He smiled and patted the alien relics, secured inside his new leather jacket. He still had time. He was going to make it...

CHAPTER 23

Logan Griff launched a furious volley of curses at the vault door as he hammered his fists against the meter-thick metal slab. However, the bolts had already thudded shut, sealing him inside.

The debilitating physical effects of whatever Hudson had zapped him with were wearing off, though his neck still burned like hell. His throbbing head was also a storm cloud of bitterness and anger, the bulk of which was directed towards Hudson Powell. Somehow, the 'dumb rook' had gotten the better of him. However, a heavy portion was also leveled at himself. He'd been sloppy; maybe even a little cocky, he admitted to himself. He should have shot Hudson the moment he set foot inside the vault, but he had wanted to lord his victory over him. It was a mistake he wouldn't make again, assuming he could get himself out of the hot mess he now found himself in. Few things motivated Griff as much as money and his finely-honed instinct for self-preservation, but his newfound desire for vengeance came pretty close.

"There's no way you're getting the better of me, you traitorous bastard!" he yelled at the door. He knew that his voice wouldn't penetrate the thick metal, but it still felt good to shout. "This is not how I go down!" he added, defiantly.

He shuffled over to where his rucksack had landed after Hudson had thrown it at him. It had been a desperate move, and Griff felt impossibly foolish for having fallen for it. He unzipped the side pocket and smiled as he removed a black case about the size of an old-fashioned paperback book. "If you really were as smart as you think, you would have taken my bag, or at least checked it first," Griff commented, still pretending that Hudson could hear him. He placed the case on the floor, unclipped the fastenings and lifted the lid to check the contents. He breathed a sigh of relief as he saw they were undamaged. Glancing at his wristpad, he noted that the new day-duty shift would arrive in just over thirty minutes. He'd have to work fast.

From the case he removed a short spool of dull-colored wire that resembled thick solder, and a blob of gray putty. Next, he grabbed a pair of dark-tinted goggles and slipped them over his head. Finally, he removed a device that looked like a small pistol and shoved it into his jacket pocket.

Scurrying over to the vault door, he applied the putty to the three lock points and pressed the wire into it in a single, long run. Pulling the goggles over his eyes, he then removed the pistol, held it an inch in front of the wire and squeezed the trigger. A searing, bright white flame that was tinted violet in the center erupted from the pistol, and seconds later the wire ignited. It burned brighter than magnesium, and despite wearing the goggles, Griff was still forced to look away and close his eyes. A few seconds later the light was gone. Griff opened his eyes and pushed the goggles up onto his forehead to inspect the effect of his work. Where the wire and putty had been there was now a glowing furrow, melted into the metal. As planned, the three bolts that held the vault door shut were now exposed.

"Damn, this alien shit really does the trick," Griff said out loud. He then quickly adjusted a dial on the pistol-like device, turning it up to the maximum setting. Dragging the goggles back over his eyes, he aimed the device at the first bolt and squeezed the trigger. The pistol released a tight cutting beam that began to slowly melt through the metal. *Come on, damn it...* Griff urged, as he moved on to the second bolt, followed by the third, each one taking a solid minute to cut through. Finally, the last bolt melted and Griff managed to pull the vault door open. Immediately, alarms rang out inside the vault room and Griff heard relays thumping. Then a cascade of lights blinked on throughout the CET presidio.

"Shit!" Griff cried out. He looked longingly at the rucksack that Hudson had filled with relics, but he knew he had to leave it behind. Its bulk and weight would only slow him down, and it would also make him more conspicuous. His sole priority now was to escape. Griff cursed again, though his words were drowned out by the blaring alarm in the vault, and ran into the corridor outside. The wail of the alarm diminished as the door to the vault room clicked shut. In its place, he heard the approaching clamor of urgent voices and the dull thud of military boots echoing down intersecting corridors. He knew the layout of the CET presidio well, and set off at a sprint towards the laundry room. If he was lucky, he'd find a uniform in there that would allow him to blend in with the rest of the grunts, like a poisonous adder hiding in the sand. He'd then slip away into the scavenger town before anyone knew what had happened.

The clatter of boots grew louder as Griff skidded inside the laundry room. Despite his height and lanky limbs, Griff moved with the swiftness and delicacy of an accomplished cat burglar. The laundry room was empty, as he'd expected it to be at this early hour. Frantically, he began to rummage through the baskets of clothes, pulling out a pair of pants and a shirt that looked like they would fit. The commotion in the corridor outside was intensifying, and he wasted no time in getting changed, leaving his other clothes buried deep in the dirty laundry pile. He'd been smart enough not to wear RGF gear, but not smart enough to have stolen a CET uniform as Hudson had done. Like his former partner's use of a skelly – a device that didn't trip the vault's alarms – Hudson's intelligent preparations for the job still grated on him. For all his taunts about Hudson being a dumb rook, he had to admit that he'd been outplayed this time.

Griff finished fastening the buttons of the CET shirt and then moved back to the door. As his bony fingers reached for the handle, the door suddenly swung open and a CET officer wearing Lieutenant's rank tabs filled the frame. Griff froze and backed away, before standing to attention, as any good CET grunt would have done. His quick thinking saved him.

"Do you not hear the alarms, Private?" the Lieutenant blurted out.

"Yes, sir," replied Griff, stiffly. He knew the less he said the better.

"Then what are you still doing in here? Get to your post!"

Griff acknowledged the order and was about to rush out, when he saw that the officer's eyes seemed to drift past him. Griff glanced back, spotting the loose bundles of clothing that lay scattered on the floor following his frantic search for a uniform that fit. It only took the Lieutenant a second to work out what had happened, but that was all the time Griff needed to crush a knee into the officer's groin. The soldier fell and Griff landed on top of him, forcing one of the loose shirts into the officer's gaping mouth. Griff then wrapped a bedsheet around the man's neck and pulled back hard. It was as if he was trying to stop a horse and cart from running out of control. The soldier struggled, legs and arms flailing around under the mass of fabric, until eventually his movements slowed and he became still and silent.

Muscles burning and gasping for air, Griff flipped over the body and quickly searched it, finding a bundle of security keyfobs attached to his belt. He unclipped the carabiner holding them in place and then removed the officer's rank tabs, attaching them to his own collar instead.

Wasting no time, Griff staggered to the rear of the laundry room. If the presidio followed a standard layout, there would be a shutter door to allow trucks to back up and collect or deliver loads. He found it exactly where it was supposed to be and cycled through the keyfobs until he hit upon one that unlocked it. Inching the shutters upwards, the sound of alarms flooded in, riding on the musky, hot air. Griff lay down and peered through the open crack. The first sun was creeping close to the horizon, but the rear courtyard was still practically deserted. Pushing the shutter up just high enough that he could roll underneath,

Griff then stood and straightened his new uniform. Taking several calming breaths, he then strode confidently towards a gate in the fence at the far end. It was guarded by a single CET private.

"Morning, Sir," the private said, throwing up a salute, before unlocking the gate.

"Morning, Private," replied Griff as stiffly as the salute he returned. He then pushed through the gate and into the scavenger town, hearing the gate click shut behind him. Once he was out of sight of the guard, he scurried into an alcove and watched as the CET presidio began to buzz with activity. Soon the compound was teeming with soldiers, all armed, all looking for the intruder that had broken into the vault and killed the lieutenant. Griff smiled, knowing their search would now be in vain. If this had been a CET presidio on a more developed inner portal world, there would have been little chance of escape. Thankfully, the caliber of soldier that was assigned to a backwater planet like Brahms Three was significantly lower. Unfortunately, Hudson had also got away, but Griff was determined to have the last laugh, no matter how long it took him.

Griff rested back against the wall and raised his wristpad, swiping across to the comms section. He highlighted a single name – Cutler Wendel – and hit 'call'. The tone whirred twice before a deep, monotone voice answered.

"Do you know what time it is?"

"Are you still on Brahms Three?" asked Griff, cutting to the chase.

"Yes. What's this about?"

Griff smiled and then answered, "I have a job for you."

CHAPTER 24

Hudson scuffed the soles of his boots on the tarmac of the spaceport while he anxiously waited to board the passenger transport to Earth. He'd already made it over the first hurdle, which was to pass through the RGF checkpoint scanner. The scanner's Shaak detectors had failed to pick up on the illicit haul tucked into the shielded compartment of Ericka's leather jacket. The five seconds he'd spent beneath the scanner's probing beams had been the most nerve-wracking of his entire life. Likewise, the relief he'd experienced when the scanner returned a negative was more blissful than a Swedish massage.

The next challenge was to actually get on board the fully-booked transport. This relied on Ma having been true to her word about punting him a ticket to Earth. However, while Earth was safer than Brahms Three, it was no more his home than the sweaty little planet he was on now. Hudson shuffled forward another couple of paces in the queue, glumly pondering his life choices. He'd never been one to put down roots, always moving from one rat-infested hostel on a portal world to another. His RGF flat in Bayview had been the closest thing he'd had to a home, even if had only been his for a few months. Now, he had nothing at all. No home, no job, and no idea what the hell he was going to do once he'd fulfilled Ericka's dying wish.

"Place your right hand on the pad and look into the ID scanner, please," said the check-in clerk. Hudson did as he was instructed, noticing that the captain and first officer were also standing behind the desk. The captain smiled vacantly at the passengers as they got on-board, as if it was some kind of Club 18-30 pleasure cruise.

"I'm very sorry, but we're already over-booked for this flight," said the clerk, apologetically. "I'm afraid you'll have to wait for the next transport in a few days, Mr. Powell."

The mention of Hudson's surname seemed to jolt the captain into action, as if someone had just shot a dart into his backside. "It's okay, Mr. Powell is a personal guest," said the captain, scuttling forward to stand next to the clerk. "He can have the jump seat in the cockpit."

"Of course, Captain Renner," replied the clerk, dutifully. He then tapped away on his console to amend the record, before printing a fresh boarding card. "Enjoy your flight, Mr. Powell," the clerk added, handing over the card, and then waving the next person forward.

"Please, come this way, Mr. Powell," said Captain Renner, ushering Hudson up the ramp and joining him by his side. "Any friend of Martina is a friend of mine." Then with a slight but perceptible raising of the eyebrow, he added, "How is she, by the way?"

"Fierce, as usual," said Hudson, smiling, "but she's saved my ass with this flight." Then he realized he should probably thank the captain too. "As have you, Captain, so you have my gratitude."

"Oh, no need to thank me," said Captain Renner, waving his hand nonchalantly as they entered the central lounge area of the transport. "Getting back into Martina's good books is reward enough for me." Then he let out an apologetic, but also clearly faked cough. "Well, almost enough."

Hudson remembered Ma's comment about sweetening the deal, and reached into the pocket of his pants for the clip of hardbucks. With his hand still in his pocket so that Renner couldn't see how much he had, Hudson deftly separated three hundred bucks. Folding the notes into his palm he then extended his hand towards the captain.

"Of course, and if there's anything I can do to help in return, just let me know," said Hudson. The captain shook Hudson's hand, deftly removing the hardbucks in the process, before sliding them into the pocket of his own pants.

"My pleasure," replied Captain Renner, now grinning broadly. "When you're ready, you can take a seat at the rear of the cockpit for takeoff. After that, feel free to wander around and enjoy the hospitality of the ship."

Hudson pointed to a circular feature at the center of the lounge, "The only wandering I'll be doing is wandering to that bar." The captain laughed, seeming to find the joke genuinely funny. Then he bid Hudson goodbye, before heading up the stairs to the top deck.

Hudson sighed, feeling another wave of relief wash over him now that he was safely on-board the transport. However, his frayed nerves were still in need of soothing, so he decided to stroll over to the bar. He hoped that he might be able to sneak in a drink or two before they departed.

Sliding onto a stool, Hudson noted that there was another man sitting at the bar, curiously without a drink in front of him. He frowned, but then called over to the barman, who was busy securing all of the bottles and glasses for takeoff. "I don't suppose I can get a quick drink before we leave?"

The barman sidled over, and raised an eyebrow, "Nervous flyer?"

"Something like that," said Hudson, which actually true in this case, though not for the reasons the barman had assumed. "I just got fired. Actually, I quit, but they fired me anyway."

"They fired you after you quit?" said the barman, clearly trying to wrap his head around how that worked. "That's one I've never heard before. And believe me I've heard a lot. What was the job?"

"I was an RGF cop," said Hudson. The barman physically recoiled as if Hudson had just declared that he was a serial murderer. "Hey, I said I *was* RGF, as in past tense! I quit, remember?"

"You also said you were fired," the barman replied, his eyes smiling. "No-one quits the RGF, but I guess you know that, already."

Hudson let out a weary sigh and nodded, "Yeah, I learnt that the hard way. Harder than you can ever imagine."

The barman scowled, but didn't press Hudson further. Instead, he ducked under the counter and returned a few seconds later with two miniature bottles of whiskey. "These were confiscated from a passenger earlier," the barman said, placing the bottles on the counter. "Technically, we can't sell them, so I normally use them to top up some of the other bottles. I get the feeling you need them more than I do."

"You couldn't be more right," said Hudson, reaching into his pocket for the hardbucks. "How much?"

The barman looked at Hudson with an expression that he could only describe as pitying.

"No charge, my friend; you look like you could use a drink. Besides, I doubt this will be the last time I see you at the bar this flight."

Hudson cracked open the top of the first miniature and downed it in one, before letting out a contented sigh. "Right again, my friend," he said, cracking open the second bottle. "And I'm a good tipper, so thanks," he added, holding up the bottle as if raising a toast. The barman smiled and continued securing his station, while Hudson sipped the contents of the second bottle. He noticed that the man on the other side of the bar had glanced across a couple of times during the exchange. He was now looking at Hudson out of the corner of his eye.

"Odd to see a man at a bar without a drink," Hudson called over to him.

"I don't drink," the man replied, flatly, "but I find that bars are where you meet the most interesting people."

He was perhaps a little older than Hudson, and had a serious, chiseled face. He had the rugged look and no-nonsense demeanor of a man who'd probably spent a lot of his time on planets like Brahms Three. Either that or he was RGF or ex-military, and Hudson felt immediately suspicious of him. Hudson didn't consider himself to have an abundance of special skills, but reading people was one of them. And even from the hunched over way this man sat, Hudson knew he was bad news.

His quiet analysis of the stranger was interrupted by an announcement over the tannoy, asking all passengers to take their seats for take-off. He necked the remainder of the second miniature and then slid off the stool.

"I often find that to be true as well," Hudson replied to the man, just agreeing for the sake of making small talk. Then he went fishing to see if he could find out anything more about him. "The name's Hudson, by the way. And you are?"

"Cutler," the man replied in a lifeless, monotone voice. "My name is Cutler Wendell."

CHAPTER 25

The sharp jolt as the transport's landing struts hit the asphalt at Ride Spaceport roused Hudson from a deep and dreamless sleep. The stresses and exertions of the last couple of days, both emotional and physical, had finally caught up with him. Combined with the effects of the two miniature bottles of whiskey, he'd been ready to pass out almost as soon as the transport had broken orbit out of Brahms Three. Unfortunately, the jump seat in the cockpit had turned out to be one of the most uncomfortable he'd ever sat in, making sleep an impossibility. Thankfully, Hudson was spared a long and unpleasant journey to Earth by his unlikely benefactor, Captain Renner. The jovial captain had graciously allowed him the use of the crew rest compartment. Captain Renner's generosity – this extra perk hadn't cost any additional hardbucks – was likely due to Hudson's

215

friendship with Ma. The captain seemed to have a mistaken belief that Hudson could influence the fierce owner of the Landing Strip to give him a second chance. While Hudson knew that this wasn't even remotely likely, he'd humored the captain in order to bank his upgraded sleeping arrangements.

Hudson slid his legs over the side of the compact bed and pulled his boots back onto his aching feet. Opening the door of the rest compartment, the Californian summer sunshine radiated inside. It was almost blinding and far more intense than the softer red hue from the twin suns of Brahms Three.

Ride Spaceport was built on the site of what used to be Vandenberg Air Force Base. This was only a short taxi-flyer ride away from San Francisco, which was Hudson's next destination. Where he would go or what he would do after that, he didn't have a clue.

A voice blared over the tannoy to announce that disembarkation would begin shortly. Hudson checked his watch, which had already updated itself to Earth Pacific Time. Out of curiosity, he looked at the local time on Brahms Three for comparison, and huffed a laugh. Considering the vast distance he'd just travelled, it hadn't been that long since he'd been standing on that hot, sweaty and dangerous world.

Hudson always marveled at how it was possible to reach a planet dozens of light years away from

Earth in about the same time it used to take people to fly half-way around the world. In fact, it often took longer to reach the territory of the Martian Protectorate than it did to reach the near-Earth portal worlds.

The clue was in the name. The near-Earth portal worlds were all accessed from the handful of portals discovered close to Earth. Each portal lead directly to another world, all roughly the same distance from the solar system. Typically, other portals could be found within close proximity to these newly-discovered planets. Threading from one portal to the next, it was possible to reach distant worlds like Brahms Three in less time than it used to take to fly from London to San Francisco.

Despite his assertion to Captain Renner, Hudson had largely stayed clear of the bar during the flight in order to preserve a clear head. Cutler Wendell, the suspicious non-drinker he'd met earlier, had been like a shadow. Had it not been for Hudson's sixth-sense for sniffing out trouble, he might not have noticed. Despite its stiff, upright seating position, Hudson had been glad of his jump seat in the cockpit. This kept him safely locked away from the passenger compartment, and from Cutler Wendell. He had absolutely no reason to suspect that this man was looking to slit his throat while he slept. Yet Logan Griff's words of warning were still clear as lead crystal in his mind. It was entirely possible, and probably even likely, that the lanky bastard had put a hit out on him. It was just Griff's style – cowardly and backstabbing.

Hudson left the crew section and thanked Captain Renner and his staff for their hospitality. Then he joined the other passengers shuffling down the exit ramp. He couldn't help but notice that everyone else looked considerably less rested than he did. This was with the exception of the few first-class passengers that had already alighted through their private tunnel.

His study of the other passengers had also alerted him to the fact that Cutler Wendell was following a few meters behind. Keen to keep a ready eye on his potential assassin, Hudson frequently glanced back as he progressed into the terminal building. In doing so, he observed that Cutler Wendell had been joined by a woman. She had the hood of a light, all-weather jacket pulled over her head, which only made her look more conspicuous.

Has Griff put two hits out on me? Hudson wondered. That would have been extreme even for Griff, he realized, not to mention expensive. They were perhaps working together, Hudson reasoned. Or perhaps his suspicion that they were hired killers was just a crazed invention of his increasingly paranoid mind. They could simply be harmless fellow travelers. He hoped it was the latter, but didn't intend to take any chances. Helpfully, since they were now back on Hudson's home turf – he'd spent three years working inter-state taxi flyers out of Ride Spaceport – he knew exactly how to lose them.

As soon as the crowds thinned, Hudson rushed ahead to put some distance between him and his pursuers. Pushing into the line, Hudson passed through the immigration checkpoint and ran out to the taxi flyer rank beyond the terminal building. Cutler Wendell was still waiting at the checkpoint, which gave Hudson the few extra seconds he needed. Scouring the registration IDs on the side of each cab, he found the one he was looking for and breathed a sigh of relief.

Checking behind again he saw that Cutler Wendell and the hooded woman had now passed through immigration. With impressive swiftness, Cutler spotted Hudson at the flyer rank, and started running his way. Hudson dashed to the taxi he'd picked out earlier, yanked open the door, and threw himself into the back seat.

"Hey, easy on the merchandise, mister," said the taxi pilot, arching his neck around to chastise whomever had jumped inside. Then the pilot saw Hudson and a broad smile dimpled his stubbled cheeks. "I'll be damned, Hudson Powell! I knew your sorry ass would crawl back here one day..."

"Good to see you too, Dex," said Hudson, reaching over and clasping hands with the pilot. "But, I need a favor, and I need it quick. Do you remember the old switcheroo?"

Dex frowned, "Of course I do, but who are you trying to lose? Are you in trouble?"

"Yes..." Hudson began, but then quickly corrected himself, "maybe. I'm not sure. But I'll explain everything later." He pushed himself back into the seat and fastened the harness. "Right now, there's a guy and a woman after me, and I need to shake them."

"You got it, Hudson," said Dex, without a moment's hesitation. Then he checked his rear-view camera and added, "Is it the serious looking dude and even more serious looking woman, jumping into Randy's flyer?"

Hudson spun around and looked out of the rear window, just catching sight of Cutler Wendell entering the cab. "Yeah, that's him, alright."

"Not a problem, hang on," said Dex, engaging the flights systems and disabling the ground brake. "I'll message Randy to hang back, and then head into the hills around Lompoc. Nadia's just up ahead too, so I'll radio and ask her to meet us in the usual place and do the switcheroo."

"Thanks, Dex," said Hudson, feeling like a blacksmith's anvil had just been lifted from his chest. The 'switcheroo' was a little maneuver that taxi flyers would employ when a customer wanted to get away without being followed. It was a problem unique to the major spaceports, due to the types of traveler that would often pass through. The typical clientele were rich socialites and shady business types. Often, they would arrive back from the portal worlds with something illicit or taxable in their possession. Whether it was to shake off the authorities or the tabloid media, Hudson had performed the maneuver many times, usually partnering with Dex or Nadia. He never expected to be needing a switcheroo himself.

"I've only got a few hardbucks on me," said Hudson, reaching into his pocket, "but I'll make good on what I owe you as soon as I can."

"Don't worry about it, Hudson," said Dex, wafting a hand in the air, "it's good to pay back a favor for once."

"Thanks, Dex," said Hudson. "It's nice to be back amongst people who aren't psychotic assholes and murderers."

Dex lifted the flyer into the air, drawing a succession of blaring horns from other flyers in the rank who had priority to lift off. He then turned southeast and accelerated towards Lompoc. Hudson checked behind again, seeing another flyer take off and start to head after them. Though the pursuing flyer wasn't moving with quite the same urgency that Dex was demonstrating.

"So, what's the deal with this duo that's after you?" said Dex, reaching cruising altitude and then accelerating hard. Hudson was pressed back into his seat until eventually Dex eased off. "Are they psychotic assholes or murderers, or both?"

"Honestly, I don't know yet," said Hudson, feeling the force pressing against his body weaken. "Let's just say my brief tenure with the RGF made me a few enemies."

"You got kicked out already?" said Dex.

"I quit before they kicked me out, actually," said Hudson, feeling it necessary to highlight the distinction as a point of pride. "But I may have pissed a few people off before that happened."

Dex's resonant laugh filled the cabin, "Sounds like you, my friend!" Then he became more serious, "I told you that the RGF was bad news. They'll hound you forever and a day now, you know that, right? No-one really ever quits the RGF. Not without consequences."

Hudson knew all about consequences. He again pictured Ericka, laughing and drinking with him in her hostel room on Brahms Three. He tried to distract himself from the memory by watching out of the window. However, he soon noticed that the scenery, as well as other flyers, were flashing past at an increasingly perilous speed. They were also only a couple of hundred meters off the deck. Hudson didn't like flying so fast or so low when he wasn't at the controls himself. Pilots made the worst passengers, he realized.

Shuffling forward in the seat, he peeked over Dex's shoulder, noting that the speedometer in the flyer was reading two hundred and ninety-eight. "I thought these flyers were hard-limited to two hundred?"

"Not this one," replied Dex, glancing back and smiling knowingly. "We'll be at the rendezvous in a few minutes, but you might have to bail without me landing."

"I hope you plan to slow down first," quipped Hudson, and again there was the resonant laugh.

An ancient CB radio crackled into life and a sparkly female voice came out over the speaker. Hudson recognized it instantly as Nadia Voss.

"Dex, I'm in position. What's your ETA, over?"

Dex picked up the old CB handset and spoke into it, "Hey there, Nadia. Expect 'the package' in sixty, over."

"I'll be ready, over and out."

"I can't believe you still use that ancient radio," said Hudson, looking at the CB unit. "Aren't you supposed to say things like '10-4 big daddy' and 'breaker one nine' or stuff like that?"

"This isn't the nineteen eighties, Hudson," said Dex. "We just use it because the cops don't monitor these frequencies, any more." Dex dropped the flyer to fifty meters and throttled back. He then expertly swung around behind a hill and headed towards an abandoned mineral mine. Hudson knew the spot well – it had been one of his popular locations to perform the switcheroo too. "We're almost there, are you ready?"

Hudson edged towards the door of the flyer and peered down towards the decaying warehouse building. He sucked in a breath and then grabbed hold of the door release. "Ready as I'll ever be."

"Okay, hang on..." Dex called out, pitching the nose forward and pulling in just in front of the warehouse. "Go, go, go!"

Hudson yanked open the door, and was hit with the powerful down-blast of air from the rotors. He edged out of the opening and then looked back at Dex, who was giving him the thumbs up. "Thanks, Dex, I owe you one!" he shouted, before jumping out of the taxi flyer. The drop was only about a meter, but he still grimaced as his boots slapped down onto the hard, tarmacked surface. The shock of the impact rattled through his bones, before he rolled forward to soak up the remaining momentum. The sleep on the way back to Earth had done him good, but his muscles throbbed and his joints still ached. "I'm getting too old for this shit..." he groaned, pushing himself back to his feet.

Dex's flyer rose up and accelerated, blasting dust and sand into his face. It was a hundred meters away before Hudson had even made it inside the warehouse building. He brushed off the sandy mineral dust and watched for a few seconds as Dex's flyer re-joined the rest of the traffic in the skyway. If they'd timed the switcheroo just right, Randy's flyer would have been unsighted for the drop-off. Dex would eventually circle back and land at Ride Spaceport again, at which point the pursuing flyer would realize they'd been had.

"Hudson Powell, long time no see..."

Hudson turned around to see Nadia Voss, arms folded and eyebrows raised.

"There had better be a bloody good reason for this..." she said, with an understated sternness that was typically British.

Hudson smiled and walked over to her, undeterred by her apparent humorlessness. As he got closer, Nadia smiled back and unfurled her arms, sweeping Hudson into a warm embrace. She planted a wet kiss on both cheeks, which she then brushed off with her fingers like an embarrassed aunt.

"I have a reason, but I don't know if it's a good one," said Hudson, drawing back and shoving his hands into his jacket pockets. "Thanks for this, I owe you one as well."

Nadia looked Hudson up and down and then folded her arms again, "I like the leather jacket, it's different for you, but a good look."

Hudson managed a weak smile, "Yeah, well it was given to me by a friend," he said, but then he hesitated and stopped. He didn't want to begin with a lie, no matter how white it was. "Actually, it used to belong to someone I cared about."

Nadia's eyebrow lifted another half an inch as she noticed the hole below the left breast pocket. "Sounds like that jacket has a story to tell..." Then looking back into Hudson's eyes, she added, "and so do you, I'd wager."

"You could say that," Hudson replied, mysteriously, while rubbing his stubbled chin. "I'll tell you all about it when we're airborne."

Nadia led them to her taxi flyer, which was neatly parked inside the warehouse building. Despite its weather-beaten decline over the years, the warehouse still provided ample cover from prying eyes.

"I take it the job with the RGF went as well as expected?" said Nadia as they strolled side-by-side.

"I quit," said Hudson, getting tired of hearing about his poor career decision, "and don't say, 'I told you so'..."

"I heard you were fired," replied Nadia, the corner of her mouth turning up ever so slightly as she said it.

"Damn it, Nadia, not you too! I quit before they fired me!"

They both laughed, though it hurt Hudson's ribs to do so.

"So, where to now?" said Nadia, sliding open the door of her flyer and inviting Hudson into the front seat, next to her.

"Back to San Francisco. Bayview," said Hudson. "There's a debt I have to pay off."

CHAPTER 26

Hudson stood on the balcony of the residential block, staring at the door of apartment forty-two where Ericka's brother lived. He'd been outside for ten minutes already, unable to muster the courage to press the buzzer. His paralysis was partly because he didn't have the faintest clue what to say to whomever opened the door. However, there was a selfish reason too. He knew that once he'd fulfilled his debt to Ericka, he'd have to face up to his own future. A future that was as uncertain as San Francisco's famously changeable weather. He knew he had to do it, but he wasn't quite ready. Not yet.

He stepped away from the door and leant on the balcony. The view overlooked the neighborhood that he'd once known as intimately as the face he saw in the mirror every day. However, despite having grown up in San Francisco in the Bayview area, it didn't feel like home to Hudson anymore. This was hardly surprising, he figured, considering that he'd left at just eighteen. He'd now spent half of his life elsewhere in the galaxy. This in itself was something that amused him, as he'd never been particularly well-travelled on Earth. In fact, he'd seen more towns and cities on other worlds than he had on his own planet.

It had been three days since Nadia Voss had dropped him off in the city. Like Dex, she'd refused to take any payment. However, Nadia had allowed Hudson to buy her a burger and a beer, so they could talk some more about his alien adventures. It was only after she'd said goodbye, giving him another polite peck on the cheek, that the sense of loneliness had really descended on him.

Despite the restaurant being busy and crowded, it was like Hudson had become invisible. He felt empty, but not from hunger, at least not in the literal sense. It was emotional malnourishment that afflicted him now. He'd never had a problem with being alone, and enjoyed and often sought out solitude more than most. Yet being alone was not the same as being lonely. He hadn't fully comprehended the difference until that moment.

In the days since Nadia had dropped him off, Hudson had employed his time usefully, and successfully. He'd auctioned off the alien CPU shards that he'd managed to smuggle to Earth in

G J OGDEN

the lining of Ericka's old leather jacket. The proceeds now sat in a new account – one that the RGF couldn't touch. The alien crystal, however, had remained tucked inside the concealed compartment in the jacket. Hudson had considered sending it to auction too, and causing a stir in the markets as a new, undiscovered relic appeared for sale. Yet while the payout could have been substantial, it would also have drawn too much attention to himself. Thanks to the Switcheroo, he'd managed to lose Cutler Wendell. However, news of a new crystal alien relic turning up in San Francisco would be too much of a coincidence to ignore. It wouldn't take much for an assassin who was well versed in the arts of detection to connect the dots.

However, it was also true that he was keen to find out more about the crystal. This was as much out of sheer curiosity as to gain a better understanding of its likely value. That was another task that would have to wait, though. To maintain secrecy, he'd need to pay a visit to a local black-market relic dealer. So, for the time being at least, the mysterious crystal remained safely hidden.

The money from the auction of the CPU shards had come in handy, given that the RGF had already emptied Hudson's bank account and repossessed his apartment in Bayview. They'd even sold off all of his possessions, which is what irked him most of all. Hudson hadn't owned any items of value, because he had never cared much for 'things'. Even so, the RGF bailiffs had peddled off everything, including heirlooms that had only sentimental value. What they couldn't sell they had incinerated, including the few family photographs he'd owned. This was seemingly for no other reason than to send a message.

He imagined Chief Inspector Wash signing off the order herself, with a gleeful flourish of her pen. He knew that she would have enjoyed such an act of spiteful vindictiveness. Sadly, he doubted it would be the last knife in the back he'd get from his former colleagues at the RGF. It seemed the rumors were true – there was no clean break from the Relic Guardian Force. *No one quits the RGF, not without consequences...* Hudson reminded himself.

Despite Logan Griff's continual jibes to the contrary, Hudson wasn't actually dumb. His time working freighters and doing courier and taxi flyer gigs had taught him plenty. Enough to make good money from the auction, and keep the profits off the radar of greedy RGF tax collectors. It was also true that he'd learned more in the last few days than in years of freelancing around the galaxy. However, while he wasn't stupid, he had certainly been naïve, and it had cost a life. The only way he was going to be able to live with that fact was by making good on his promise to Ericka. It wouldn't wipe the slate clean, but it would at least allow him to start a new chapter.

His previous flying gigs had also furnished Hudson with plenty of contacts who were good at tracking people down. The key was finding Ericka's personal records, and in particular her surname. This had turned out to be 'Reach' – Ericka Reach. With a name that unusual, and the foreknowledge that her brother lived in Bayview, finding him hadn't been difficult. However, it had still taken a full day for Hudson to walk up to the door, which he was now standing outside, procrastinating.

"Come on, Hudson, get a grip," he spoke out loud into the foggy morning air. "Let's just get this over with..."

He took a deep breath and then returned to the door, but it was almost impossible to press the buzzer. It was as if the gravity acting on his hand had suddenly intensified tenfold. Then the decision was made for him, because the door suddenly opened, and the aggravated face of a man stared back at him.

"Look, can you stop loitering outside the damn door. I'll be out of here as soon as I can," the man immediately protested. "The last guy that came said I could have two more days, and it's only been a few hours!"

Hudson noted that the man was propped up by a crutch, and wore a hefty back and leg brace.

Through the door, he could see a couple of kids — a girl and a boy, both perhaps six or seven. They were playing on the floor of the lounge, which was completely empty, save for a couple of toys and two small duffle bags.

"I'm not a bailiff, I'm not here to kick you out," said Hudson. His mouth was dry and his voice wobbled like a buoy on a rough sea.

"Then what do you want?" said the man. He was curt, but not rude. Then he gestured inside the apartment and added, "If you're selling something then I'm afraid you've come to the wrong place."

"I'm not selling," said Hudson, "I was a..." he thought carefully about his next word and chose, "...friend of your sister, Ericka. You're Kelvin, right?"

Kelvin Reach's face fell at the mention of his sister's name. He glanced back to check on his kids, before gently pulling the door closer so that they couldn't see the stranger outside. "Look, they don't know yet, and I've got a lot of other crap to deal with right now. I don't want to sound cold, but..."

Hudson held up a hand, "I understand. I won't keep you for more than a minute." Then he reached into his jacket pocket and brought out a credit scanner. "Press your thumb to this."

"I told you, I don't have any money to buy..." Kelvin began, but Hudson cut across him.

"I'm not selling, I'm transferring," said Hudson, pointing to the display. Kelvin's eyes landed on the number and his confusion only deepened, as did the frown lines on his forehead. "Ericka got a big score on her last hunt. I was with her when she cashed it in. So, this is all yours."

Kelvin's eyes danced from the display on the pad to Hudson's and back again, "But is it all...?"

"Yes, it's all legal and accounted for," Hudson lied. He didn't like lying, but this time it felt good. "She told me about you and your situation, and so after she..." Hudson paused and forced a dry, hard swallow, before continuing. "...I mean, after what happened, she asked me to find you and make sure you got this. So here I am."

"But who are you?" said Kelvin, "Are you a hunter too? How did you find me?"

"Like I said, I was a friend of Ericka's," said Hudson. He now badly wanted to leave. Far from being cathartic and soul cleansing, the experience was only dredging back up the traumatic events he'd tried so hard to bury. "That's all there is to it. Now, press your thumb on the pad, and I'll be on my way."

Kelvin hesitated again, but Hudson raised the scanner to his hand and looked at him. His eyes implored the man not to ask him any more questions. Kelvin's lips quivered, and he appeared to be considering probing Hudson further, but instead, reluctantly, he pressed his thumb to the pad. The transfer completed and Hudson placed the credit scanner in Kelvin's trembling hands.

"There's enough there to buy this place, if you wanted to," said Hudson, "and plenty more besides. Enough to get you back on your feet."

Kelvin was still struck dumb, and so Hudson took the opportunity to leave. However, he only made it a couple of paces, before guilt stabbed at his chest. He pressed his hand to the leather jacket, feeling the outline of the crystal in the hidden compartment, and then turned back to Kelvin.

"There's also this," said Hudson, slipping the crystal shard out of the compartment and showing it to him. Under Earth's yellow sun, it glistened and shimmered in a way no earthly object did. Kelvin stared at it, almost hypnotized by its ethereal hue.

"What is it?" he said, transfixed. "It's stunning; I've never seen anything like it before."

"Very few people have," said Hudson. "Your sister found it on one of the alien wrecks. So far as I know, it's the only one of its kind. It could be worth a lot." He held out the crystal, offering it to Kelvin. "You should have it too."

Kelvin took the crystal and turned it over in his hands, admiring its unearthly beauty. "Look, you've done so much for me already," said Kelvin, offering the crystal back to Hudson. "You could have taken this money for yourself, but you didn't. I don't know what planet you come from, but I don't know anyone on Earth who would do what you've done."

"Maybe you just need better friends," said Hudson, smiling, but the joke was also an attempt to deflect the compliment. He didn't feel particularly virtuous. He'd handed Kelvin the money as much to salvage his own conscience as to do the right thing by Ericka.

Kelvin managed a weak smile in return, "You're probably right there." He pressed the crystal back into Hudson's hand and closed his fingers around it. "But I don't need this. And I think she'd want you to have it. Maybe you can work out what it is, and write yours and Ericka's names into the relic hunter history books."

Hudson almost said, 'Oh, I'm not a relic hunter...' but he realized that this would just open a can of worms. He didn't want to get into a discussion about his past with the RGF, as it would inevitably lead onto how Ericka died. And that was a conversation he didn't want to have. Instead, he accepted the crystal and placed it back inside the compartment in his jacket.

The commotion of squabbling children then distracted Kelvin's attention. He peered back inside the apartment where his two kids were now fighting over one of the few toys they had left. "I'd better get back inside," said Kelvin, nodding in the direction of the warring siblings. "Plus, I need to make a few calls and credit transfers." He extended a hand to Hudson, and added, "Thanks to you, I just got my life back. Ericka was lucky to have a friend like you, and I don't even know your name."

"I'm no-one, just an outcast of society, trying to do the right thing," replied Hudson. "And I was the lucky one. I'm still alive." Then he reluctantly took Kelvin's hand and shook it. "I'm sorry I couldn't bring her back to you too."

The two men said their goodbyes and Hudson left the apartment, ambling slowly back along the balcony to the stairwell. He was in a virtual dream state as he began to descend slowly to street level. He didn't notice the silver-haired lady pass by him on the way up, carrying a brown paper bag full of groceries. He didn't notice the ginger cat sitting on a windowsill, pausing mid-wash to regard him with curiosity. And he didn't notice the surveillance drone humming in near silence outside, tracking his every move.

CHAPTER 27

Handing over the credits to Kelvin had lifted a weight from Hudson's mind, but he still had a heavy heart. *It should have been Ericka doing this, not me...* he told himself. It wasn't just her senseless death that weighed on him, it was also the injustice of how it had happened.

Hudson had a clear sense of fairness, and he'd always done right by people and his friends. Even when it became clear that the RGF was as crooked as he'd been warned it was, he still did things 'by the book'. He remembered how Griff had relentlessly mocked him for using that phrase, and then it dawned on him why he was still so angry. Griff had spent his career swindling and thieving, under the mentorship and authority of another swindler and thief. And he had no doubt that Chief Inspector Jane Wash reported up the chain to ever more crooked superiors. Griff had flouted the rules

237

with regularity and he'd always seemed to get away with it. Hudson had bucked authority once and it had gotten Ericka killed. It wasn't fair. It wasn't right. And that pissed him off.

In an attempt to clear his head, Hudson went for a walk down towards Hunter's Point, close to where his own apartment had been. Seeking solitude, he wandered into a deserted area of old warehouses. It was an area that was designated for the future expansion of the RGF base, but as usual budget cuts had delayed its construction. He found a tattered old bench, brushed off some of the peeling paint and sat down. A few minutes later, a ship launched and then blasted into orbit. He couldn't help wondering whether the crew on board included an idealistic rookie like he had been. Another 'dumb rook', foolishly believing that the RGF existed to ensure fair play. Hudson wondered if they would be tainted by its corruption and become just another Logan Griff or Jane Wash.

The light was fading and the air was turning colder, so Hudson decided to head back into Bayview. He was getting hungry, and he considered going to one of the soul food places off third street. However, as he left the bench and turned away from Hunter's Point, he caught a glimpse of a shadow moving behind one of the condemned buildings. The area was deserted apart from him, and it was hardly a romantic spot for lovers to take a stroll. The hairs on the back of his neck tingled and he suddenly felt vulnerable and exposed. *Perhaps someone saw or overheard me showing the crystal to Kelvin?* Hudson wondered. He hadn't noticed anyone else around, but he'd also hardly been discreet about mentioning the crystal's potential value. If anyone had been snooping behind twitching curtains, they might have overheard.

Hudson adjusted his route back in order to put some distance between himself and the shadows. He hurried, while still trying to walk as normally as possible, and cut through a side-street. Quickening his pace, he checked behind as the thud of boots thumping against the asphalt grew louder. Two figures flashed past the entrance to the side-street and continued on the road parallel to where Hudson was now headed. In a few hundred meters, he'd be back on busier residential streets. He knew the area like the back of his hand, and was confident he could slip away unseen. However, he assumed that his pursuers would know this too, and so would choose to make their move soon.

Hudson quickened his pace again, almost to a jog, keeping the abandoned warehouse between him and the shadows. He scanned the ground around him, looking for anything he could use as an improvised weapon. It might not come down to a fight, he realized, but Hudson wouldn't be caught unprepared again. From now on, he was going to fight first and ask questions later.

A cut-off run of copper pipe lay abandoned in a pile of rubble and he swooped down to pick it up without stopping. Gripping the bar tightly he stepped up another gear and fixed his attention on the end of the wall, which was approaching rapidly. Then, through a crack in the tinted glass windows of the warehouse, he saw the shapes flash past again. They were running across the top side of the building to where Hudson would soon emerge. His heart thumped in his chest, but this time he wouldn't be caught off guard, not like he had been by Griff in the CET presidio. Giving himself over to pure, gut instinct, Hudson charged ahead in the hope of cutting off their ambush. Then just as he reached the top end of the warehouse a man darted out, weapon raised, and Hudson recognized him immediately as Cutler Wendell.

Cutler's eyes grew wide as the copper pipe swung towards him and then slashed down across the side of his head. It made a crisp, almost musical chime as it connected with his skull. Cutler fell hard and the pistol tumbled from his hand, but his accomplice was only a fraction of a second behind. Adrenalin was pumping through Hudson's veins, heightening his reactions and speed. No sooner had the bar rung against Cutler's head than he'd swung it towards the second attacker. Cutler's accomplice, face shrouded under a dark hood, raised a forearm just in time to block the brunt of the blow. Quick reactions saved them, but the accomplice was still buffeted back against the wall of the warehouse. Hudson pressed his advantage and swung again, but this time his opponent was ready. The hooded figure dodged the blow and then grabbed Hudson's arm, trying to wrestle the bar from his grasp. Hudson resisted and managed to push his opponent away, like two attracted magnets being torn apart by force. However, the copper bar had slipped from Hudson's hand and clattered across the road. He raised his guard and prepared for another round, but then he saw that his opponent had drawn a weapon and raised it at him. It was an antique single action revolver. Hudson frowned, recognizing the weapon, and looked up at his attacker. The hood had been pulled back, revealing her face clearly for the first time. It was a face he'd also seen before. It was the face of Tory Bellona.

CHAPTER 28

Hudson lowered his guard a fraction and stared at Tory over the top of his fists. "What the hell are you doing here?" he yelled at her, and then he glanced down to Cutler Wendell, still out cold on the cracked asphalt. The answer was obvious, but he didn't want to believe it, "Wait, don't tell me you're with him?"

"I'm not *with* him..." Tory answered, holstering her pistol. She stressed 'with' as if to highlight her disgust at the suggestion that Cutler and she might be more than just partners in crime. "I work for him, that's all."

"And I'm your job?" cried Hudson. "So, you're what... a hitwoman? I thought you were a damn relic hunter!"

"I am, but I'm also what Cutler needs me to be," Tory hit back, her eyes taking on a harder edge. "It's complicated."

"But, why? Why are you trying to kill me?"

"I don't know," said Tory, shrugging. "I don't ask, and I never care. Some pig RGF cop hired him, that's all I know."

"Griff..." said Hudson, the word passing through his teeth like poisonous gas. He dropped his guard fully and straightened up, looking Tory dead in her steel blue eyes. "So, what now, Tory? Are you still going to kill me?"

There was an excruciating silence that only lasted a few seconds, though it felt like hours, until Tory Bellona finally answered, "No."

Hudson felt like every muscle in his body suddenly went limp. Though his pulse was still racing like he'd just run a marathon. "Well, that's good to know," he answered, testing to see if a little sarcasm might soften Tory's razor-sharp edges.

"Not this time, anyway," Tory added darkly, not responding to Hudson's attempt to lighten the mood. "I owe you for Brahms Three. Rex would have cut me down, given half a chance, but you stopped him. That's something I won't forget." Hudson was about to speak up again, but Tory wasn't done. "But don't get any ideas, mister. I owe Cutler more than I owe you, and he won't let this slide. Especially now you've made him look like a damn fool, not once, but twice."

Hudson rubbed his chin wearily and nodded. It was clear that this wasn't going to be the last time he dealt with Cutler Wendell.

"So, when he wakes up, is he just coming straight after me again?" asked Hudson, glancing at Cutler to make sure he was still out cold.

"Not straight away, no," answered Tory. "We have other places we need to be."

Hudson raised an eyebrow, "A hitwoman's work is never done, eh?"

This time there was the faintest quiver of movement at the corner of Tory's mouth. However, if she had found Hudson's retort amusing, she was trying hard not to show it.

"He'll lick his wounds for a time," Tory went on, "but he won't forget, I promise you that."

"And when he does eventually come after me again, will you be with him?" asked Hudson. He wasn't sure whether he was asking because he wanted to see Tory again or because he didn't. The fact this made Hudson feel conflicted just confused him even more.

Tory nodded, "Yes."

"So maybe I should just kill him now," declared Hudson. He had used his best poker face, but Tory just laughed dismissively.

"We both know you won't do that. You're not like him, or me."

"Seems to me that you're not like him either," replied Hudson.

Tory's jaw tightened and her eyes grew even sharper. Hudson could almost feel her gaze slicing into his skin. "You don't know me, Hudson Powell, and you don't want to know me. I'm dangerous. I'm a killer. And you should stay out of my way, like I told you back on Brahms Three."

"From what you've said, it seems like I may not have a choice," answered Hudson, sharpening his response to match. "But – and don't take this the wrong way – I hope I never see you again." The answer was supposed to sound tough-talking, but it actually came off sounding the opposite.

Do I want to see her again? He asked himself, still trying to wrap his own head around what he was feeling. It was like getting stung by a scorpion and then wishing it would scuttle back over and sting you again.

Tory didn't respond, but Hudson could see her eyes had softened. It was only by a touch, like a puff of color on a stark white canvas, but it was enough to tell Hudson that there was a side to Tory Bellona beyond violence and extortion. Then her brow suddenly furrowed, wrinkling her satin skin.

"Who was the man you visited in the apartment block up in Bayview?"

The question threw Hudson off guard, and he blabbed a response, eager to keep Kelvin off Tory's radar. "What? What man, I don't know what you're talking about."

Tory's expression hardened like diamond again, "That was a lie – you only get one."

Hudson felt a shiver run down his spine – Tory's warning was genuinely chilling. He thought for a moment, weighing up whether or not to trust her. On the face of it, a deadly relic hunter turned assassin sounded like the last person on Earth – or any other planet – that Hudson should confide in. Yet for some unfathomable reason he trusted her.

"Okay, but you have to promise me you'll leave him alone. I don't want him involved."

"I told you, I don't make promises," said Tory.

"This time, you have to," Hudson hit back instantly, staying locked onto Tory's eyes, which burrowed back into his own. Neither blinked, neither wavered, until eventually Tory broke the stalemate.

"Okay," she said, reluctantly. "I promise."

He's the brother of someone I knew on Brahms Three," Hudson began, "Someone that your employer killed. I was paying a debt, that's all."

Tory's eyes narrowed, "A friend?"

"Fine, she was a little more than a friend," admitted Hudson, remembering Tory's warning. "But that's not why I came here. I don't expect you to understand."

"I understand just fine," Tory replied, acidly, sounding genuinely affronted. "And what about the crystal – did you already know about that when we met in the alien wreck?"

Hudson had not anticipated this question, and he knew that his poker face wasn't good enough to conceal another lie. Besides, Tory seemed to have the ability to cut through bullshit like a plasma

246

torch through chocolate. She'd obviously seen Hudson with the crystal, so lying to her would only turn a reluctant enemy into a vengeful one.

"Yes, I already knew about the crystal when we met. But I didn't have it at that time."

Tory nodded and continued to hold Hudson's eyes for another few seconds. Then she turned away and recovered Cutler's sidearm from the asphalt. Hudson felt terror grip him, realizing he may only have seconds to live. However, instead of pointing the weapon at Hudson and firing, Tory held it out towards him.

"I don't want that," said Hudson, relieved to still be alive, but also perplexed by the strange offer.

"When Cutler wakes up, he'll want to know why I didn't take you down," said Tory. Then she added with a cool certainty, "Because believe me, if I'd have wanted to, I could have taken you down."

The macho side of Hudson wanted to argue back, but recent experience had taught him when it was best to simply shut up.

"So, you're going to have to shoot me," Tory continued.

"What?!" yelled Hudson. "I can't shoot you, are you mad?"

Tory pressed the weapon into Hudson's hand and then backed up against the wall of the warehouse. "My clothing is reinforced, so the bullet won't penetrate through." She then stood tall and smoothed down her jacket. It was the same slim-fitting, rugged-looking garment she'd worn when they'd met in the wreck on Brahms Three. Then she pointed to her left side, "Hit me here and I'll be just fine, bar a broken rib or two."

"Are you sure?" queried Hudson, glancing at the spot Tory had indicated. The jacket certainly looked tough, but it didn't look like it would stop a bullet. "It's a hell of a risk."

"It's only a risk if you can't aim," Tory hit back, "Just shoot already."

Hudson raised the weapon, but he was still far from convinced, despite Tory's bravado. And it was clear that she could see the doubt written plainly across Hudson's face.

"Shoot me, damn it!" Tory snarled.

Hudson gritted his teeth and aimed the weapon, "I'm sorry..."

Tory braced herself. "If I see you again after this, you will be."

Hudson almost laughed, but just managed to hold it together, before he added pressure to the trigger and fired.

CHAPTER 29

Hudson sat in a bar in the India Basin, nursing another drink. It had taken a full thirty minutes, plus two beers and bourbon chasers for him to stop shaking after pulling the trigger on Tory. The animal, caveman part of his brain told him to run and leave town. However, he had enough presence of mind to listen to his better judgement. If he ran, taking a flyer or booking a transit out of San Francisco, he'd leave an imprint that Cutler might be able to trace. After all, he'd managed to track him to the city, despite the 'switcheroo' that Dex and Nadia had pulled off.

It was only after his third shot of bourbon that Hudson had the gut-wrenching apprehension that Cutler may have gotten to Dex and the others. Hudson didn't want to risk calling Dex directly, in case Cutler was monitoring their frequencies. However, he had been able to confirm the registrations of all active taxi-flyers operating out of Ride Spaceport in the barman's epaper. The cabs belonging to Dex and Nadia were still active. It wasn't a guarantee that either was still alive, but it was enough to make Hudson feel more relaxed about remaining off grid. Lying low was his best option, at least until he could be reasonably sure that Cutler and Tory had moved on. He knew his reprieve was only temporary; Cutler would be back.

As for Tory Bellona, Hudson's aim had been true, as were Tory's claims about her reinforced jacket. However, the impact of the bullet had still jolted her against the crumbling concrete, almost knocking her out. Hudson attentively checked her over to make sure her injuries were not life-threatening. Luckily, other than a concussion and – as Tory had predicted – a couple of cracked ribs, she had been okay. Hudson had not enjoyed the experience of shooting Tory at near point-blank range. However, he was certainly grateful that he wasn't going to be around when the fearsome relic hunter fully regained consciousness. The phrase, 'like a bear with a sore head' came to mind. Except that Tory was more panther than bear.

Hudson finished his drink and then held out his hand, palm facing the counter top. The alcohol had finally dulled his nervous system to the point where he had stopped shaking. Dropping some hardbucks onto the bar, Hudson headed out into the street. It was already starting to get dark, but he had another stop-off to make, before he moved on. *Move on to where?* Hudson asked himself, realizing he still didn't have anywhere to go. That was a decision that would have to come later, though. Right now, he needed to find a very special kind of establishment. And, unlike the bar he'd just left, with its conspicuous neon sign, this was a place that could only be found if you already knew where to look.

Hudson had learned of the place in question while auctioning off the alien CPU shards. Helpfully it was only a couple of streets further up towards Bayview. He found the unmarked black door of the quaintly-named 'Antiques & Curiosity Shoppe' and pushed through. Inside the compact, eccentric store were floor to ceiling glass shelves. The shelves were packed full with oddities from all over Earth and the portal worlds. Nestled amongst the Earthlier artifacts were some alien relics, most of which even Hudson knew had more novelty value than anything else. However, Hudson also knew that the items and services of true worth in the store were not the ones on display.

"We're closed" said a bald man, who was resting on the counter top at the back of the store. He was scrutinizing a silver cube that was about the size of a six-sided die through a magnifying eyepiece.

"I need you to do an examination," said Hudson, ignoring the store owner's curt greeting.

The bald man looked up, still wearing the magnifying eyepiece, which made one eye appear to balloon up like a boiled egg. "If you're looking for a doctor, you're on the wrong street..."

Hudson was already tired of playing games and so cut to the chase. He reached inside his leather jacket and pulled out the alien crystal. It glistened with an unearthly radiance under the store's bright lights, as if it was absorbing the energy of every bulb in the room.

The bald man removed the magnifying eyepiece and stared in wonder at the crystal. It was like Hudson had just drawn Excalibur from the stone and presented it to him. Then without another word he reached under the left side of the counter and pressed a button, locking the door and tinting the outside window black.

"Seven hundred and fifty for the initial assessment," said the bald man, with a haughty air of superiority. "Five if paying in hardbucks. And, if you choose to move the item through these premises, I take twenty-five per cent of the final sale value."

Hudson snorted a laugh and shook his head gently. *Twenty five percent... this asshole's even more of a crook than Griff.* He may have escaped from the clutches of the RGF, but it seemed that when it came to alien relics there was no escaping

252

from money-grubbing vultures. And black-market dealers like this man were amongst the most predatory.

Hudson approached the counter and placed the crystal on the surface. He then reached into his pants pocket and pulled out a clip of hardbucks. He'd already burned through what had remained of Ericka's stash, but he'd taken some of the value of the relics he'd auctioned off as cash instead of credits. Credit scans could be tracked – hardbucks could not. He counted out five hundred, which was most of what he had left, and held it out.

The dealer took the money and placed it in a metal tray below the counter. He then unlocked a large metal cabinet and placed an assortment of fantastical-looking contraptions on the counter top. He worked feverishly to set it all up, talking excitedly as he did so.

"I have heard of this crystal," he began, "word of its finding travelled fast, even from Brahms Three. It was thought to be a myth, or simply lost, but here it is, in my Shoppe!"

The store owner picked up the crystal delicately between his forefinger and thumb. He admired it for a moment, before securing it above one of the contraptions with a pair of thin metal tongs.

"Such a find is remarkable indeed," the man went on, "I already have a theory as to what it may be." Then he switched on the apparatus, which thrummed softly as the energy built up within it.

The crystal lit up from the inside and began to pulse, almost as if it were a living, beating heart.

"Hey, are you sure you know what you're doing?" asked Hudson, eyeing the relic anxiously. It looked like it might spontaneously explode, taking him and half of the Western United States with it. "It looks kinda dangerous..."

"No, not at all," said the dealer, dismissively, while studying a raft of data flooding onto his computer screen. Then he seemed less sure of his own assertion, "Well, not dangerous to humans, in any case."

"That's hardly reassuring..." said Hudson, starting to regret his choice to get the crystal assessed. He wished he'd spent the five hundred back in the bar instead.

"It's putting out a truly phenomenal amount of Shaak radiation," the relic dealer continued, enthusiastically. "Genuinely, I do not know how this is even possible."

Hudson raised his eyebrows, "Just how much radiation are we talking here?" He had instinctively taken a pace back, as if that would somehow offer some protection.

"My dear sir, Shaak radiation is harmless to human beings," the relic dealer said, patronizingly. "Though, I must confess I've not seen a modulation quite like this before." He looked up at Hudson and smiled, "It appears that, like the crystal itself, this radiation signature is unique."

"That's great, but it sounds like what you're really saying is that you don't know what the hell it is," said Hudson. He wanted a concrete answer out of the dealer, one way or another.

"No, I don't know what it is, not with any certainty, at least," the dealer admitted. He appeared to be both embarrassed and annoyed with Hudson for pointing that out. "But I believe that it may be some form of transceiver," the dealer went on. "Or at least a core component of a device that the alien vessels may have used to communicate with one another. Perhaps even through the very portals themselves, as it appears to share a similar signature."

"That's some hypothesis," said Hudson. He was genuinely intrigued as to the crystal's function, but he was also keen to learn whether it was actually valuable. "But is that worth anything?"

The dealer looked at Hudson as if he'd asked, 'is fire hot?'. He ran his hand over his smooth head and smiled, "My dear sir, we may be talking about the ability to communicate almost instantaneously with all the portal worlds. No relays, no time delays. This could perhaps be the key to live, real-time communications with people dozens of light years away, as if they were no more distant than you are from me right now. It may even be able to control the portals in some way." The relic dealer wiped his hand over his mouth, as if someone had just put a juicy steak in front of him. "I would dearly love to study this some more."

Hudson raised his eyebrows and blew out a low whistle. "So, it's pretty valuable then?"

The man smiled politely. "Somewhat, yes." Then he powered down the equipment and removed the crystal from its clamp, placing it delicately on the counter. Hudson observed that the dealer had placed the crystal closer to himself than to Hudson. "However, it also appears to be damaged, or at least incomplete."

Hudson frowned. The fact that the dealer had kept the crystal close to him told Hudson that he was definitely interested in it. This meant that the suggestion it was damaged could simply be a bargaining tactic. Hudson was no stranger to bartering, having been forced to barter for fuel, spare parts, landing permits and more during his many years flying around the galaxy.

"Looks fine to me," said Hudson, refusing to fall into the dealer's trap. "Besides, you've never seen one before, so how can you know it's damaged?"

The dealer pointed to a section at the top of the crystal and then highlighted a scan of the area on his screen. "There..." he said, pointing his carefully manicured finger at the screen. "You can see a lip around this area and a small indentation. It appears to me that there is a piece missing." Then he shrugged his shoulders and did his best to appear disinterested, "Which of course affects its value..."

Hudson smiled, recognizing the tactic well, but the bald dealer's poker face was worse than his own. "Even if that's true, this is still the only example in the entire universe. So, I'd say it doesn't affect its value at all." Then Hudson hit back with some barterer's logic of his own. "If there was only one Monet left in existence, would you turn it down because of a little tear in the canvas?"

"Personally, I would," replied the dealer, snootily. "I detest Monet." Hudson rolled his eyes. "But... I do enjoy alien relics, even damaged ones," the dealer was quick to add. "So, I am prepared to personally offer you four hundred."

Hudson actually laughed out loud; the offer was worse than a slap in the face. "Four hundred? I just gave you five!"

The dealer smiled, "Four hundred thousand..."

Hudson's eyes almost popped out of this head. Four hundred thousand would set him up with a new life, or even buy him his own ship. He was sorely tempted, but the dealer had offered too much, too quickly, which told Hudson that the likely value of the crystal was far higher. If he could confirm the dealer's hypothesis then he realized it could be worth significantly more.

And he also found himself thinking about the dealer's suggestion that the crystal was perhaps incomplete. *What if I could find the missing part?* Hudson thought to himself. *What if I could unlock its secrets?* He realized that he found the prospect of discovering more crystals and secrets far more exciting than the money. Money would buy him things, but he didn't care for things. What he truly needed was a calling. He felt a tingle run down his spine at the thought of adventuring throughout the galaxy. Finding the missing part of the crystal would mean Hudson hunting for it himself inside the alien wrecks. It would mean he'd have to become a relic hunter. The only problem was that he didn't have a ship, and the only way to get one was to sell the relic.

Hudson sighed and then reached over the counter. He grabbed the crystal and placed it back into the compartment inside his jacket. The dealer's face fell as he did so, as if he were a kid and Hudson had just taken away his favorite toy.

"I'll think about it," said Hudson, tapping his breast pocket. "Thanks for the information."

"You are declining my offer?" the dealer replied, his polite smile suddenly vanishing.

Hudson could sense that the dealer's demeanor had shifted. He realized that he'd misjudged the bald man's sudden change of mood. He wasn't saddened that Hudson had taken back the relic, he was outraged. It was like a cat suddenly switching from being friendly and playful to lashing out with a frustrated claw.

"I said I'd think about it," replied Hudson. He appeared calm on the outside, but inside he was mentally steeling himself in case the dealer decided to pounce.

"Very well. Then I will just buzz you out," the dealer continued, reaching down beneath the counter top.

Hudson followed his hand down, watching as it slid underneath the right-hand side of the counter top. This was the opposite side to where he had activated the button that locked the door initially. Whatever the dealer was doing, he wasn't letting Hudson leave.

The dealer then sprang a weapon from under the counter top, but Hudson was ready. Before the bald man was able to aim the barrel in Hudson's direction, he'd already caught his wrist and stripped the weapon from his grasp. The dealer's mouth fell open with a sudden, shock realization that his plan had been foiled. However, his gaping jaw was quickly shut again as Hudson clocked him on the chin with a hard left cross. The dealer went crashing backwards into a metal shelving rack, before crumpling into a heap on the floor. An assortment of oddities tumbled on top of him.

Hudson recovered the weapon that the dealer had pulled on him and examined it. It was a shock pistol; non-lethal, but it packed enough charge to have put him down. After that, who knew what the black-market dealer had in mind. Hudson shuddered, knowing that he'd again come close to a grisly demise.

Hudson reached over the counter and pressed the correct button. The door unlocked and the tint was removed from the window. "On second thoughts, I've decided to decline your gracious offer," said Hudson, as the dealer pulled himself back up, covered in glass and broken curiosities. Then Hudson grabbed the five hundred hardbucks he'd handed over earlier from the metal tray. He wasn't a thief, but he sure as hell wasn't going to let the vulturous dealer keep his money. "This is for trying to rip me off," said Hudson, waving the money at him. "You're lucky it's all I'm taking."

"I conducted your assessment!" the dealer protested, "That money is mine!"

Hudson smiled and then flipped the safety off the taser pistol. "No, this is yours..." he replied, tapping the frame of the pistol with his free hand. "And you're going to get it." Then he aimed at the dealer's chest and pulled the trigger.

CHAPTER 30

The barman quietly sidled up in front of Hudson, who was sitting on a stool at the bar. It was a different watering hole to the one he'd visited before heading to the Antiques and Curiosity Shoppe. However, it shared the same neon-lit exterior and slightly sticky floor.

"Give me something wet and strong," said Hudson, catching the barman's eye. "And leave the bottle."

The barman's eyebrows raised up, before he fetched a bottle of bourbon and a single tumbler. "I think I'm going to need to add to my next wholesale order of liquor..." he said, placing the items down on the solid oak counter top.

Hudson smiled, "What can I say, I'm a barman's best friend."

The barman filled the tumbler and left the bottle, which had barely returned to the counter top before Hudson had necked the shot.

"You look like you have a few stories to tell," the barman said, while topping up the glass.

Hudson looked at the timid contents of the chunky tumbler. He yearned for a few shots of Ma's volcanic whiskey instead. "I don't suppose you have anything stronger?" he asked, glancing hopefully at the barman.

The barman raised an eyebrow, "Yeah, I do, though I mainly only use it for de-greasing the grills."

"Sounds perfect," said Hudson, before necking the second shot.

The barman's other eyebrow lifted, "Okay, son, it's your funeral," he said, and then disappeared below the counter. There was the sound of glass bottles chinking together, mixed with a few curt profanities as the barman struggled to reach whatever he was looking for. Then he finally re-emerged and blew a layer of dust off a dark-colored, square bottle. He fetched two clean glasses and poured a couple of generous measures.

"Let me guess," the barman said, picking up his glass. "You're just back from the portal worlds. Relic hunter, right?"

Hudson sighed, before picking up his glass and downing the contents. It was like liquid fire, though still not a patch on Ma's insane elixir. He placed the glass down and thought about how to answer the question, "Yeah, something like that."

The barman frowned and then downed his shot, though unlike Hudson, he spent the next few seconds thumping his chest and wheezing. Hudson smiled, "It's good stuff, right?"

"Only if you like killing brain cells," replied the barman. He then slid the bottle towards Hudson as if it were a deadly poison he wanted out of his reach. "Help yourself, there's no-one else in here crazy enough to drink it."

There was a call from the other side of the room, and the barman waved a response. He then grabbed a credit scanner and dropped it in front of Hudson. Hudson frowned at the scanner, knowing he didn't have a credit to his name. Instead, he pulled out the stack of five hundred hardbucks he'd reclaimed from the dishonest dealer. He separated out a few of the notes and placed them on the counter.

The barman picked them up and looked at them like they were alien artifacts, "Well shit, I don't see these much anymore. I might struggle to find you any change."

"Hudson tapped the square bottle on the counter, "Don't worry, we'll call it even."

"Hardbucks and hard liquor, huh?" replied the barman, shoving the notes into his breast pocket. "It must be some kind of crazy-ass life out on those portal worlds. When do you head back out?"

Hudson poured himself another drink from the dark bottle. Despite everything, he really did want to get back 'out there'. Perhaps the whiskey had nulled his sense of danger, but he wasn't afraid. Even the close-shave with the dealer, or the knowledge that Griff and Cutler were still gunning for him didn't deter him. The thought of heading out to a distant portal world and seeking adventure inside an alien wreck was no less intoxicating than the liquor in his glass. He'd joined the RGF because he believed it was what his father had wanted. Since then, he'd had plenty of time to ponder his choices. He now knew that he'd confused his father's message. 'It doesn't matter what it is, just make sure it matters to you, okay?' his father had said. *Make sure it matters to me...*

"Well, I kind of have a transportation problem at the moment," said Hudson, finally answering the barman's question.

"What sort of problem is that?"

Hudson grinned and then necked the shot, "I don't have any transportation."

The barman laughed, before grabbing an epaper, and sliding it next to the anonymous bottle of liquor. "You're in luck, there's a shipyard out by Hunter's Point with a sale on." Then he tapped a finger on the epaper to activate it. "You can read the details in here."

"Thanks," said Hudson, drawing the epaper closer. He swiped through the pages until he found the advert the barman had mentioned.

"Owner is a damn crook, of course," the barman went on, "A guy called Swinsler, if you can believe that. Swinsler!" There was another impatient shout from the other side of the bar, and the barman yelled back, before turning again to Hudson. "Anyway, I'll leave you to your de-greaser. And if you do make it back out there, good hunting."

Hudson poured another shot and raised the glass, "Good hunting," he repeated with gusto, before downing it. The effects of the potent beverage were beginning to take their toll, and he was starting to lose feeling in his toes.

The barman left and Hudson found himself alone with a half-empty bottle. For lack of anything else to do, he read the ship sale advert in the epaper again. It irked him that he had no hope of affording anything without selling the crystal. However, selling it would deny Hudson his chance of discovering its mysteries. Maybe it was because of Ericka, or maybe it was for some other reason he couldn't yet comprehend, but uncovering the crystal's secrets actually mattered to him.

He flipped idly through the other pages of the epaper until he found a departure board for Ride Spaceport. He scanned through the list of ships' names and captains, wishing that his name could have been among them. Then one entry caught his attention. It read, 'Ship Registry: Hawk-1333F | Captain: C. Wendell | Departed: 22:54 | Destination: Unspecified.'

"I hope you crash and burn, you bastard," Hudson said out loud. Then he remembered that Tory was most likely also on-board and mentally retracted his wish. He knew he shouldn't do, but he really liked her. *Perhaps that's just the whiskey talking again...* he mused.

Hudson took the bottle and the epaper to a table and slumped down on the comfier, padded seats. He removed his leather jacket and dumped it on the seat to his side. The jacket flopped open, revealing the inner compartment and the tip of the strange alien crystal, and he cursed himself for being so careless. He tucked the crystal back inside, but then noticed that another, much smaller object was also peeking out. Hudson reached in and removed it.

"I'll be damned," said Hudson, turning the object over between his fingers. It was a high-grade alien CPU shard; one of the relics that he'd smuggled off Brahms Three. Hudson guessed that he must have missed sending it to auction along with the others because of its size. Based on the prices the other shards had fetched he reckoned that the little high-grade processor was worth a good amount. Maybe even enough for a small ship. It wouldn't be anything fancy, even compared to the stripped down RGF Patrol Crafts, but it would be a start.

Technically the profits from selling the CPU shard belonged to Ericka's brother, Kelvin. However, Hudson was content that he'd settled Ericka's debt in full. Kelvin and his family were going to be just fine, but what about Hudson Powell? Didn't he deserve another chance?

He slipped the shard back into the compartment, pulled the jacket back on and wandered outside the bar. It was close to midnight and the sky was clear and pitch black, save for the bright pinpricks of light piercing the veil of nothingness. He wandered along the road, head swimming. This was partly because of the liquor, but mainly because of the choice he'd just made. He stopped near a junction, before the road descended towards Hunter's Point. A ship had just launched from the RGF base and was quickly soaring out of sight. Reaching inside his jacket, Hudson removed the little CPU shard again and looked at it.

"Do something that matters to me..." Hudson said, soaking in the chilly sea breeze. He then carefully placed the shard back inside his jacket and fastened it up to block out the cold. "Hudson Powell, relic hunter..." he spoke into the night air, testing to see how it sounded. It sounded pretty damn good.

Hudson turned away from Hunter's Point and began to stroll down the middle of the deserted street towards Mission District. He had no destination in mind, but hoped to stumble past a hotel or guest house along the way. If nothing else the walk would give him time to sober up, because tomorrow he would need a clear head. Tomorrow, he would sell the alien CPU shard. Tomorrow, he would head back to Hunter's Point to buy his own ship. And tomorrow, he would finally do something with his life that he actually gave a shit about. Tomorrow was the day that Hudson Powell would become a relic hunter.

The end.

EPILOGUE

The pulse of Shaak radiation emanated out from the Antiques and Curiosity Shoppe, and began probing through space. Drawing energy from the power lines and sub-stations spread across San Francisco, the intensity of the pulse grew exponentially. And then it was abruptly shut off.

Deep in space above Earth, a portal began to resonate in unison with the crystal's alien rhythm, before passing its beat to another. Soon, every portal that humankind had ever found sang in harmony with the crystal's song. As did all of the portals that had remained undiscovered.

Within a matter of hours, the pulse had travelled throughout the galaxy, passing through portals like neurons transmitting impulses through synapses in the brain. Eventually the signal had permeated deep enough into the galactic core to reach a vessel that had lain dormant for eons. Greater even than the titanic hulks that lay broken across dozens of sterile worlds, this goliath vessel was not a ruin. And its task was not yet done.

The pulse seeped into the vessel's circuits, like rain water filling cracks in the desert. Gradually the great ship was restored. After countless millennia, it finally knew where it was. More importantly, the great ship also knew where it must go.

At last it would fulfil its function. At last it would purge the corporeal species that had infected system 5118208. The rage that had been trapped within its cavernous shell for thousands of years could finally be unleashed. It once again had a purpose.

Goliath would soon emerge from the darkness. And this time, nothing would stop it.

TO BE CONTINUED

The Star Scavenger Series continues in book two, Orion Rises.

Orion Rises:

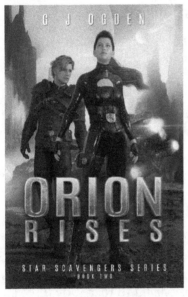

READ THE OTHER BOOKS IN THE SERIES:

- Guardian Outcast
- Orion Rises
- Goliath Emerges
- Union's End
- The Last Revocater

ALSO BY THIS AUTHOR

If you enjoyed this book, please consider reading The Contingency War Series, also by G J Ogden, available from Amazon and free to read for Kindle Unlimited subscribers. Also available as an audiobook on Amazon, Audible and iTunes.

- The Contingency
- The Waystation Gambit
- Rise of Nimrod Fleet
- Earth's Last War

"Highly recommended - sci-fi fans will not be disappointed with this novel."
Readers' Favorite, 5-star review.

No-one comes in peace. Every being in the galaxy wants something, and is willing to take it by force...

ABOUT THE AUTHOR

At school I was asked to write down the jobs I wanted to do as a 'grown up'. Number one was astronaut and number two was a PC games journalist. I only managed to achieve one of those goals (I'll let you guess which), but these two very different career options still neatly sum up my lifelong interests in science, space and the unknown.

School also steered me in the direction of a science-focused education over literature and writing, which influenced my decision to study physics at Manchester University. What this degree taught me is that I didn't like studying physics and instead enjoyed writing, which is why you're reading this book! The lesson? School can't tell you who you are.

When not writing, I enjoy spending time with my family, walking in the British countryside, and indulging in as much Sci-Fi as possible.

You can connect with me here:
https://twitter.com/GJ_Ogden
www.ogdenmedia.net

Subscribe to my newsletter:
http://subscribe.ogdenmedia.net